AF487381

# Lambda

## The story of life between two points.

Kapil R. Sharma

All rights reserved:

It is illegal to republish, copy, distribute, reuse, photocopy, record or by any other mechanical or electronic means any part of this publication without the prior written permission of the author. All rights of this book are reserved by the author.

---

Disclaimer:

All the characters and stories in this novel are completely fictitious. Any resemblance of any incident or character described in this novel with any living or dead person will be considered a mere coincidence.

Cover Page- Ms. Vandana Vashisht

# Contents

# Introduction

Someone once told me during childhood that if you asked something of the birds returning to their nests in the evening, you would get it. The only condition was that you had to truly want it. I believed in that, and today, after so many years, when I look back, I find some truth in it. I received what I desired, though its form had changed.

Every person, at least once in their life, encounters the question of what they have gained and lost in life. Often, the answer only comes after a long time, when one can look at their past with a neutral mind. Sometimes, the answer to this question is revealed only in the final moments of life. When a person sets out on a journey toward a destination, it's not always certain they will reach it, or they may reach it but not under the circumstances they had envisioned.Life doesn't give anything easily—love, money, power, fame—everything comes with a price. And that price changes a person. It alters the meaning of the results of their efforts.So far in my life, this is what I have discovered. I have hundreds of stories and memories connected to such experiences, which I have always wanted to organize into written form. Due to a lack of time, this hasn't been possible. But if you feel alive, the voice of your inner soul continues to resonate, and slowly, it gets the work done.

**Acknowledgements**

The first suggestion to turn this story into a book came from my elder brother, Sanjeev Kumar. He has been involved in the production of films like *Madaari* and *Daas Dev*, featuring Irrfan Khan, and he strongly believes in creative dialogue. Like a mentor, he has always inspired me to pursue creative writing, and he even directed the short film *Dwandwa* based on a script I wrote. It was his faith that made me feel I should complete this novel.

I don't know how successful I have been in this attempt, as I am not a great writer. It wouldn't be right for me to dwell too much on what people will think of my writing, how they will critique it in terms of grammar and literary style. What I do know is that I write what I feel and try to give it words. While writing this novel, the only thought in my mind was that whoever finishes reading it should feel a positive energy in their life—an energy that gives them the courage and strength to move forward. If that happens, it would be the success of my writing and the success of this novel.

I first dedicate this book to my late grandmother, Mrs. Maheshwari Devi, my grandfather, Mr. Brahmdutt Sharma, and my wife, Meghna. My childhood up to my youth was spent with my grandparents, and it's impossible for me to separate that from myself. I have known Meghna since school days, so I have spent a long part of my life with her. These three people have been the guides of my life. Guidance is not just about what they did for me, but it also depends on how I shaped my path because of them.

My mother, Mrs. Manju Sharma, and father, Mr. Rajesh Sharma, have always blessed me, and without their blessings, no work is ever possible. I took time away from my children, Nimitt and Vedangi, to complete this book, so they, too, have been major inspirations behind this effort. Additionally, my sister Jyoti and brother Mukul, who are themselves involved in film and TV writing, have always encouraged me in my writing.

I would like to express special thanks to Vandana Vashisht for the beautiful illustration on the cover of this book. At the end,with the blessing of Goddess Saraswati, I dedicate this book to all of you readers. I hope you will like it and that it will touch some aspect of your life.

**Kapil R. Sharma** *Patna 12.02.2023*

# Chapter-1

Manoj sat quietly, away from the crowd in the field, tearing off some strands of grass and pressing them between his teeth. People often do this when they sit alone—sometimes as a result of deep thought, and other times simply out of boredom. Manoj ran a small grocery store, or what people nowadays call a "general merchant" shop, where he sold items like candies, biscuits, and household groceries to make a living. His shop had a limited number of customers, and many times he would sit for hours waiting for a good customer to make some decent sales. It was in his shop that he realized that waiting for customers could feel longer than waiting for a lover. In a small grocery store in the village, eyes often tire from waiting for customers, and only on rare days do fortune and a good sale coincide.

Manoj didn't have enough capital at the time to start a bigger business, and no other path in life seemed promising enough to risk everything on. As he sat in the field, the taste of grass spread over his tongue. After spitting out the dried pieces, he would pick new strands and resume chewing.

The field was bustling with activity, with people from dozens of nearby villages gathered around. The event was being held because the upcoming Panchayat elections were near, and the block head had organized a series of games to garner attention and support. Various sports competitions were scheduled for the entire day, and soon, the 1500-meter race would begin.

The chief guests for the Panchayat Games were the local MLA and the SDM. Manoj had always been interested in sports and even earned a Bachelor's Diploma in Physical Education during his studies, though he never pursued a career in that field. Out of this interest, he had closed his shop early that morning to come and watch the games. Although Block Head Ranveer Singh Yadav had studied in the same village school as Manoj, life is never defined by who you were—it's about what position you hold today. Now, Manoj was the tired owner of a small, customer-starved grocery store, while Ranveer was a political figure, hailed by the people. The difference between them was clear. Manoj watched the block head and other dignitaries seated on the stage from a distance.

That day, many runners from far and wide villages had come to compete. Some boasted of being able to run from their village to the city, while others claimed they could start running at sunrise and not stop until sunset. Some claimed to outrun cheetahs, while others said they outpaced horses. The air was full of exaggerated boasts, almost as if there were a contest of braggadocio.

Yet, amidst this noise, there were also serious athletes whose silent demeanor reflected their determination. It's often said that the real champions are those who don't speak much. The audience's main interest lay in the 1500-meter race because the winner was promised a large fridge, and the runner-up would receive a big cooler. At that time, owning a fridge was a status symbol—having cold water on a hot day was like nectar, and neighbors would ask for ice or water, feeling indebted to the fridge owner.

The cooler, too, had its own significance; Without a cooler, sleep seemed restless, as if broken by heartache. This was the late 1990s, a period where the world wasn't as fast as WhatsApp, nor as slow as a bullock cart—life was somewhere in between, caught in transition, as history was about to take a sharp turn. Back then, letters sent by post often got lost, but technology was advancing rapidly with the arrival of Pager, SMS and email. Now, messages could be sent far away in just moments.

That day, significant preparations were made for the 1500-meter race. The race was to start within the field, pass through a specially constructed kilometer-long track outside, and end back inside the Panchayat grounds. A large number of people had gathered to watch the race. The villagers were lined up on both ends of the marketplace. The SDM, the chief guest, had arrived, so the police were deployed to ensure no disruptions. Ropes were tied on both sides of the road to keep anyone from stepping into the track during the race.

Amidst all this hustle and bustle, Manoj found a quiet corner where he could see the entire competition. A voice from the microphone on the stage announced, " ladies and gentlemen, Hold your breath, the biggest race of the year, the 1500-meter race, is about to begin in just a few moments. Jitendra Kumar, the winner from last year's Hakkan Kheda village, is here again. Let's see if Jitendra Kumar can win this time, or will someone else take the crown? Remember, friends, only those with the guts can reach the sky... If you think you've got it, get ready to race and register your name with the head clerk of the panchayat office near the tent."

Manoj watched silently with disinterested eyes. A few familiar faces from the village bumped into him, but Manoj had no desire to talk to anyone. When the heart is heavy, solitude is often the only comfort, and conversations feel like an unwanted burden. Just then, two girls approached Manoj. Lakhaniya and Baby both knew Manoj from before and were from the same village as him. Baby's father raised pigs, and Lakhaniya's father worked as a daily wage laborer. Both girls also worked for a few families as a domestic help and would go early in the morning to sell the vegetables grown in those fields at the nearby town market. Their settlement was on the outskirts of the village, where they lived with other families from their community.

The two girls stood in front of Manoj. Still sitting on the ground, Manoj glanced at the girls and, showing no interest, looked back at the stage set up for the chief guests in the field. Seeing no initiative from Manoj, Baby nudged Lakhaniya to speak to him. Mustering up some courage, Lakhaniya spoke.

"Bhaiya, Ram-Ram," said Lakhaniya.

Manoj, looking at both the girls, replied, "Ram-Ram."

Lakhaniya asked, "Brother, can girls not run in this race?"

Manoj looked surprised and asked, " Do you want to run?"

Lakhaniya replied, "For the prize."

Manoj asked, "What is the prize?"

Both Lakhaniya and Baby pointed toward the prizes kept in the tent.

Baby said, "Whoever comes first in the race will get a big fridge, and the second place will get a cooler."

Now Manoj could also see the fridge and cooler kept for the winners in the tent.

"What will you do with a fridge and cooler?" Manoj asked.

Lakhaniya replied, "We'll enjoy cool air and drink cold water. The heat of Jeth (summer) burns our skin, and we can't even sleep at night."

Manoj laughed, "Oh, silly girls... even if you win the fridge and cooler, where will you get electricity? Do you have a connection at home?"

Baby responded, "The line has come to the part behind the village; if needed, we'll get the connection from Puttan uncle's house."

Manoj, hearing Baby's reply, said, "Puttan is a sly guy; he won't give you the connection. He follows caste discrimination strictly."

Lakhaniya said, "Brother, first let us win, and then we'll figure out how to run the fridge and cooler."

By now, Manoj was getting irritated, and he didn't like the disturbance in his solitude.

"This is a race for boys; girls don't run in this," Manoj said. "Now leave."

Hearing this, Baby and Lakhaniya felt disheartened and turned back, mumbling. As they walked away, Baby said, "They won't let us run, and then they'll say girls are weak." Her murmurs were loud enough to reach Manoj's ears. Hearing this, Manoj paused for a moment and then called out to the girls.

"Hey, girls, listen!"

Baby and Lakhaniya turned around. Manoj signalled them to come back, so they walked back to him.

Manoj said, "Alright, let me see what I can do. I didn't know feminism had reached the village." (Manoj muttered to himself.)

Lakhaniya and Baby didn't understand what Manoj meant by feminism, as they were unfamiliar with such a heavy word. They were just happy that Manoj was going to register them for the race. Their eyes sparkled with hope. For the first time in the history of that village, Manoj and these two girls were about to do something that would be recorded as a significant event.

Anyway, Manoj took both girls to the registration tent, where names of the participants were being registered. The registration counter was crowded, and Bada Babu (head clerk) was writing down names, addresses, ages, and village information in a register along with two other men. There was chaos at Bada Babu's desk. People were pushing over each other. Most of them were anxious not to miss the chance of winning the fridge and cooler. Some had just come to participate without any real intention. Serious athletes were laughing at the commotion, wondering how they would have to compete with these fools.

One boy, wearing shorts, shouted so loudly, "Hey, register my name too, Bada Babu!" As soon as he finished, another boy started yelling, "Hey, register both me and my brother, Bada Babu!"

Bada Babu turned toward the two boys and asked, "What are your names?"

The boys told their names in order.

The older brother said, "Aatma Kumar."

The younger brother said, "Parmatma Kumar."

Bada Babu stopped writing and looked up at them, asking again, "What did you say your names were?"

The older brother repeated, "Aatma."

The younger brother repeated, "Parmatma."

Bada Babu, now convinced, said, "Aatma, Parmatma."

The boys confirmed, "Yes."

Bada Babu asked, "So your father named you Aatma and Parmatma?"

The boys replied, "Of course!"

Bada Babu burst into laughter with a tone of sarcasm, and moving the conversation forward, said, "Then surely there must be 'Moksha' at your house too."

The boys were confused and asked, "Who's Moksha?"

Bada Babu replied, "Well, if Aatma and Parmatma are in the house, then Moksha must be there too, right?"

The boys, embarrassed, replied, "No, there's no Moksha. We have four sisters."

Bada Babu asked, "What are their names?"

The boys replied, "Pooja, Archana, Vandana, and Aarti."

Bada Babu, unwilling to miss the opportunity for more fun, immediately quipped, "Looks like your father is a deeply religious man. He's practically set up a temple in your house!"

Then Parmatma spoke, "Our father has taught us how to give blessings too, (Bada Babu) head clerk. Write the names, or i'll have to offer blessings." This comment stung the head clerk. "Give me the blessings, then. Go ahead; let's see how you manage to get names registered here." The boys also chimed in, "Why won't you write the names? Is it your inheritance? You have to write the names." The sarcastic remarks from both sides somehow escalated into tension. The commotion grew louder, and just then Manoj shouted, "Write their names or not, but make sure to write these two names: Lakhaniya and Baby."

Hearing this, the head clerk lowered his head and wrote in the register, muttering, "After soul and spirit, now we have Lakhaniya and Baby too. These villagers sure give their kids strange names. Where are you, Lakhaniya and Baby? Come forward."

The two girls came forward with Manoj. The head clerk exclaimed, "These two are girls!"

Manoj replied, "So, what's the problem?"

Head Clerk: "This race is for boys. Will these girls run alongside the boys in half-pants?"

Manoj: "They will run, as long as no one has a dirty mind. There's no separate race for girls here in the village, so they'll run with the boys."

Another man standing nearby commented, "This competition for a fridge and cooler, what all it will make people do!"

Head Clerk: "No, girls can't run with boys."

Manoj: "They'll run with their feet. Are the boys running with their hands?"

Head Clerk: "Oh, come on, don't argue with me. I don't have the energy for useless fights. The officers are sitting inside; go talk to them."

Manoj realized the head clerk was being stubborn and wouldn't understand quickly. So, without wasting time, Manoj briskly walked toward the stage where the chief guests and organizers were seated. As he was heading that way, the Block Pramukh (chief) Ranveer, who was also organizing the village games that day, stopped him.

Ranveer had been watching the drama unfold from afar and was worried that no new commotion should arise in front of the SDM (Sub-Divisional Magistrate), the chief guest. To control the situation, Ranveer spoke to Manoj, "What's the matter, Manoj? Have you come to run too? Good, you'll get in shape. Sitting in the shop has made you soft."

Manoj: "No, I'm not here to run. I've come to register two names, but the head clerk is telling stories and refusing to write them."

Ranveer: "Oh, who are these people? Let's see what champions you've brought..."

Manoj: "These two girls are here to run, but the head clerk won't write their names. He says they can't run with the boys. Manoj suggests organizing separate games for the girls, but if there are no games for them, what are they supposed to do? Just clap for others?"

This remark made Ranveer slightly angry. "Why are you waving the flag of women's empowerment? Let the women raise that flag themselves. If it doesn't happen this time, we'll organize games for girls next time. Now, go from here."

By then, the SDM had also walked over. Hearing Ranveer's response, Manoj felt agitated.

Manoj: "But this time, the girls are missing their chance. You leaders always talk about gender equality, but then discriminate like this. Is this fair?"

Ranveer: "You talk as if these girls are PT Usha, about to fly in the air once they start running. The boys have been preparing for weeks; how will they match up? What if they lose? Then what will happen to your pride?"

Saying this, Ranveer turned away to greet the SDM without waiting for a response. Just then, Manoj's voice came from behind, "And what if they win? What will happen to the boys' pride then?"

This remark hit Ranveer hard, and without turning back, he instructed, "Head clerk, and write both girls' names. There's great joy in establishing social justice, and this gentleman here wants to savour that joy to its fullest."

# Chapter 2

After stepping down from the stage, Manoj felt a mixture of fear and satisfaction. He feared that the girls probably wouldn't win, but at least they were getting a chance to run. In our villages, it's no small thing for girls to get equal opportunities.

Meanwhile, the announcement from the stage echoed loudly: "In today's race, two girls will also be running with the boys. So, stay till the end and witness this historic event." Hearing this, a large crowd gathered to watch the race. In society, whenever girls do something that challenges men, it inevitably becomes a matter of curiosity. And when it's about physical strength, the interest only intensifies.

Manoj was feeling both joy and concern at the same time. It's a feeling one often gets when they know they've done something right but remain uncertain about the outcome. Baby and Lakhaniya, walking beside him, whispered to each other. Manoj asked, "Do you have shoes?"

Lakhaniya replied, "No."

Curious, Manoj asked again, "No shoes?"

Baby retorted, "Why do you keep asking about shoes, brother? Are you planning to hit us by shoes?"

Manoj hadn't expected such a reply. "No, you fools! I'm asking so you can run. How will you run?"

Lakhaniya replied, "We'll run barefoot."

Baby added, "We'll manage to run, but brother, you made such big statements there. What if we lose?"

Hearing this, Manoj paused for a moment and said, "You're not world champions, are you? If you lose, you lose. We'll smile and walk away.

The fact that two girls dared to run in a boys' race—now that's an achievement."

Lakhaniya: "Still, people will make fun of us."

Manoj: "If they do, we'll wrap a scarf around our heads and head back home. Let them talk nonsense—who cares? We've already faced enough in life. If you girls are losing courage, let's go back and cancel your names.."

The girls replied, "We're not losing courage, brother, but this is the first time we're doing something like this. Our legs are shaking a bit."

Manoj: "The first time you do anything, your legs will shake. But if you push through it, you'll achieve great things. Have you heard the story of Trijata?"

The girls: "No, brother."

Manoj – Near Ayodhya, there lived an extremely poor Brahmin named Trijita in a forest. He survived by digging up soil. Due to extreme poverty and many days without food, his body had become frail and weak. With his frail body, he had lost his self-confidence and had stopped going to the city and other rural areas to ask for alms. His life was filled with hardship, and his wife and children often went hungry for days.

One day, Trijita's wife advised him to go to Lord Rama and explain his situation to ask for some alms. Following his wife's advice, Trijita set out to meet Lord Rama in Ayodhya. By coincidence, it was the very day that Lord Rama was about to leave for his exile and was distributing all his wealth before his departure.

Trijita narrated his tale of poverty to Lord Rama. Then, Lord Rama told Trijita, "Pick up your stick and throw it with all your strength. I will give you all the cows that your stick passes over."

Hearing this, Trijita thought Lord Rama was mocking him, making fun of his weak body. Some of the people present there also began to laugh at him. Determined, Trijita vowed to throw the stick with all his might. Girding his loins, he hurled the stick into the air with all his strength. The stick flew over the Sarayu River and landed far beyond a herd of about a thousand cows grazing on the riverbank. Everyone present was astonished to see the indomitable strength of Trijita's frail body.

Lord Rama embraced Trijita and said, "Brother, do not be upset by my condition. I just wanted you to believe in your extraordinary strength. For humans, self-confidence is their greatest weapon. With self-confidence, even in weak situations, with limited resources and challenging circumstances, one can achieve extraordinary things."

After narrating this story, Manoj asked the girls, "Did you understand? You can give up many things, but never give up your self-confidence. You both are brave, which is why you've come here with this determination. Now leave the result up to God. Like Trijita, recognize your inner strength and run with all your might."

As Manoj was saying this, the competitions on the field had already begun. Shortly after, an announcement from the stage was made, "The next competition is the 1500-meter race, and today, two girls from Biswa village, Baby Kumari and Lakhaniya Kumari, will race along with the boys. Moments like these rarely happen in history, so we request the audience to stay until the race is finished. All participants are requested to take their positions on the track."

Soon after, Baby and Lakhaniya stood on the track alongside the boys, ready to race. Manoj observed the two girls standing there in their worn-out salwar and pajamas, their eyes fixed straight ahead on the track. Their hair, filled with dust, shimmered brown under the sun, but there was something special in their eyes—fearlessness. It didn't seem like they were about to do something they had never done before.

Despite this, Manoj was wondering whether these girls could complete the 1500-meter race when the whistle blew, and the race began. The moment had moved beyond thinking. In the next instant, Manoj could already predict the outcome. He saw that all the boys had surged ahead, leaving the two girls trailing behind. Manoj wasn't surprised by this result; he had expected it. He was only relieved that the girls wanted to participate, and had it not been for his efforts, they might not have even taken part. Block head Ranveer's words seemed to ring true—but Manoj was agree that working for social justice brings a satisfaction that overshadows personal losses, and even if the outcome isn't a success, the joy of attempting to establish justice remains.

All participants had to run first lap of 400 meter around the field and then head to the outer track of 700 meter before returning to the final lap of 400 meter in the field. The boys had already moved onto the outer track, and Manoj could see the two girls lagging far behind, making their way out.

The special thing about this race was that the outer track was not visible to the audience seated within the field. In rural areas, such improvised tracks are still used for organizing sports competitions. Meanwhile, the commentary continued from the stage, "All runners have moved onto the 700-meter outer track, and once they complete it, they will return to the field for the final 400 meters."

As the commentary continued, Manoj heard the audience murmuring, waiting for the runners to return to the field. Then, someone approached and informed Manoj that he had been called to the stage.Ranveer was seated on the stage. When Manoj arrived, Ranveer said, "Manoj, do you remember how our master used to tell us the story of the singing donkey when we were kids?"

Manoj said nothing.

Ranveer – In a village, there was a farmer who had a donkey. Along with farming, the farmer also kept cows and sold their milk. The donkey had the illusion that he was an excellent singer and was always looking for an opportunity to sing. However, the farmer didn't like the donkey's singing at all and would scold him whenever he tried. But the donkey was obsessed with singing. Eventually, the donkey became friends with two cats. The cats were very clever; they thought they could take advantage of the donkey by listening to his singing and, in return, sneak into the farmer's house to drink the milk.

One night, while the donkey was singing, the two cats quietly slipped into the house and started drinking the milk from the pots. However, the donkey got so carried away with his singing that he began braying loudly. The noise woke up the farmer and his family. When the farmer saw that all the milk, meant for sale the next day, was ruined by some animals, he became furious. After searching the entire house, the two cats were found in the donkey's shed. The farmer quickly understood that the donkey had brought the cats into the house under the pretence of singing. Enraged, the farmer picked up a stick and beat the donkey. When the donkey returned to the cats after being beaten, the cats also kicked him away.

The moral of the story is that one should not indulge in foolish actions; otherwise, consequences come from all directions. Hearing this, the people around Ranveer burst into laughter. However, Manoj decided not to respond, as he did not want to escalate the situation. But Ranveer, on the other hand, was determined not to miss the chance to pull Manoj's leg.

Ranveer – "Hey, before saying or doing something, think about the outcome. Now look, your cats fizzled out, and you ended up as a musician. You shouldn't say things that embarrass yourself."

Manoj understood that Ranveer had called him over just to humiliate him, and he had been prepared for it. But just before Manoj could respond, he heard the voice of Bada Babu.

Bada Babu – "Look over there, sir!"

Everyone's attention turned to the track where runners were returning after completing the final 400 meters. Seeing the scene, Ranveer was left speechless, and to everyone's astonishment, everyone on the stage stood up. The crowd in the field erupted in excitement. Manoj looked back to see what was happening and saw a boy entering the field to complete the final lap, with another boy close behind, followed by a third, and then a fourth.

Before Manoj could fully grasp the situation, he noticed something that had made the people on the stage stand up: behind the fourth boy, Baby was sprinting like lightning, with Lakhnya storming behind her like a whirlwind.

One by one, all the boys were being left behind. When the race had started, there were fifty runners, and Baby and Lakhaniya were at the back. But now, everything had changed. The voice from the stage announced that the final 400 meters of the race remained and that the two girls had completely turned the tide. For the first time in the history of village sports, girls had not only participated in a race with boys but had also left them gasping for breath.

In a few moments, the result of the race would be revealed. Baby and Lakhaniya had pushed all the boys behind, with only two boys remaining ahead, who were now quite close. At any moment, Baby and Lakhaniya could overtake them. The final 200 meters were left. Baby and Lakhaniya ran so fast that all the "cheetahs" were left eating dust, their feet moving at a speed as if they were not running a 1500-meter race but a 100-meter sprint. Seeing this, a spark lit up in Manoj's eyes. For him, it was like witnessing a transformation, like a mouse shedding its skin to reveal a lion inside. Filled with excitement, Manoj rushed to the edge of the track, raising both hands to cheer for the girls.

There are moments in life that can change you instantly, forcing you to face a truth you may have forgotten in your despair, believing nothing would ever change. But these moments rewrite the story in unexpected ways. For Manoj, this was such a moment. He had not anticipated such a surprising race.

He continued to cheer loudly, raising both hands, as the two girls crossed the finish line ahead of all the boys. Amid the loud cheers, Manoj covered his face with both hands. His eyes were closed, his mind went blank, and the noise of the crowd gradually faded away, making him feel like he was falling asleep standing up.

At that moment, Manoj felt as if everything around him was happening slowly, like a rocket that had suddenly halted just as it was leaving Earth. Then he heard the sound of a train speeding on the tracks, the "clatter-clatter" sound of the rails. As he focused on the sound, he imagined a train racing forward.

All the general and sleeper compartments of the train were packed with passengers. People were sitting wherever they could find space, crammed into every inch. Even the floor and the bathroom were full, with people leaning on each other as the train sped towards its destination. From one such crowded compartment, a boy was crying in the bathroom.The half-closed bathroom door suddenly opened, revealing a boy wiping his tearful eyes. His eyes were red from crying. Quietly, the boy stepped over the passengers sitting on the floor and made his way to where he had placed his bag, saving his spot. He picked up the bag and sat down. The people around him were so packed that they were practically sitting on top of each other. The boy buried his head in his lap, resting on his bag.

As the race in the village field reached its final moments, Manoj was lost in his subconscious, trying to recognize the boy sitting with his head on his bag. After a few moments, the boy's face became clear. In that semi-conscious state, Manoj realized that the boy was himself. As soon as he recognized the boy, the sound of the train on the tracks grew louder, faster, and even more intense.

# Chapter 3

In Delhi, India Gate was built by the British in memory of the Indian soldiers who fought on their behalf in World War I. Near India Gate is the Rashtrapati Bhavan, the residence of the President, who is the first citizen of the country. Flanking Rashtrapati Bhavan are the North Block and South Block, from where the country's administration is run. Delhi also houses the Parliament, where laws governing the country are made, the Red Fort, and the Supreme Court. However, there is another place that holds a special place in the hearts of the young aspirants who come to Delhi with dreams—Dholpur House. This is the office of the Union Public Service Commission (UPSC), the institution that selects officers for the Indian Civil Services, including IAS, IPS, and other central services.

In the middle class, becoming an IAS or IPS officer is often seen as the most prestigious way to attain power and glamour. A young man might go to bed as just another aspirant one night, but if he clears the IAS exam the next day, he wakes up as a "Lord Sahib." In an instant, he gets money, a house, a car, servants, a bungalow, a beautiful wife, authority, power, respect, and glamour, all at his fingertips.

There's someone to open the car door, someone to close it, someone to carry his diary, and someone to set up a chair for him wherever he goes. Families line up to offer their daughters in marriage, and everyone around him calls him "Sir." No other profession offers such a staggering return on investment for the middle class, and if one can "extract oil from sand," as the saying goes, they can secure the future of their next seven generations. This is why the middle class stakes everything on it—if you succeed, you've hit the jackpot.

At a tea stall, Pintoo Ji was sipping tea with one hand and holding a samosa in the other while speaking continuously to a group of half a dozen young men who had come to Delhi to prepare for the IAS exam. One of the boys interrupted him, asking, "But what does it take to 'extract oil from sand'?"

Pintoo Ji replied, "Nothing much, just one exam. You just have to pass this one exam. It's not just an exam; it's a battle for life. If you win, the world is yours, the glory is yours, history is yours."

The boy responded, "But the real question is, how do we pass this exam, brother?"

Pintoo Ji said, "Just like our Lord Bhola Bhandaari does it. My roommate, Manoj, he is at Dholpur House today, giving his interview. Once he becomes an IAS officer, whether I make it or not, I'll maintain my status back in our neighborhood."

All the boys were excited. After all, who wouldn't want to hold the hand of a hero already on the path to realizing his dreams?

The boys chimed in, "Brother, please introduce us to Manoj Bhaiya someday; it will be a blessing for us."

Pintoo Ji replied, "Sure, brother, I'll introduce you soon."

As he said this, Pintoo Ji reached into his dirty jeans pocket, which hadn't been washed in two weeks, to pay for the tea and samosas. "Oh damn, my wallet's back at the room!"

The boys said, "No worries, brother, we'll pay."

Pintoo Ji, shaking his head, said, "No, no, I should have paid for the tea." The boys laughed, "No problem, brother, just introduce us to Manoj Bhaiya, that will be enough."

Pintoo Ji burst into laughter, "Oh man, you guys are too much... don't worry, Manoj is my best friend. I'll introduce you whenever you want."

The boys nodded in respect.

A few hours later, as evening was approaching, footsteps could be heard on the stairs leading to the roof of a four-story building. Someone wearing shoes was rushing up. The door to the roof opened, and a young man wearing those shoes emerged, leaning against the wall to catch his breath. Several young men and a few women were already standing on the roof. Pintoo Ji had also arrived earlier.

Seeing the young man trying to catch his breath, Pintoo said, "What's up, Manoj? You're late! I thought you'd go straight from your interview to your posting in Nagaland. Where were you?"

Everyone laughed at Pintoo's comment. But Manoj had only one question: "Has Pooja arrived?"

Vivek, another friend of Manoj, assured him, "Yes, she came with me. Where were you? We've been waiting for you for ages."

Manoj replied, "I was just having trouble finding a ride." At that moment, a voice called out from the other end of the roof. It was Pooja.

Pooja: "How was your interview?"

Manoj: "How did yours go?"

Manoj had asked both Pooja and Vivek. Everyone else was also standing around, eager to hear how Manoj's interview went. After catching his breath and taking a sip from a water bottle, Manoj asked Vivek, "What did they ask you?"

Vivek: "They asked me what I've studied, and then they asked some questions from my subject, Political Science, like why fundamental duties aren't mandatory, why citizens are keen on receiving fundamental rights but show indifference towards fulfilling their duties as per the Constitution. They asked if I thought fundamental duties should now be made compulsory. After that, they asked me about tribal development in Madhya Pradesh, the political obstacles in Indian economic growth, and administrative policies for poverty, illiteracy, and tribal development."

Everyone went silent for a moment, thinking about the answers they would have given if they had been asked the same questions. Some even wanted Vivek to share the answers he gave to the interview board. But before that could happen, Pooja began to speak.

Pooja: "They asked me about my service preference. They pointed out that I chose IAS as my first preference and IPS as my second, whereas many female candidates opt for the Indian Foreign Service as their second choice. They asked why I didn't."

Pooja shared not only the questions but also the strategy behind her answers.

Pooja: "I told them that I wanted to work within the country, staying connected with the people and working for them directly. Then they asked if I thought that Indian Foreign Service officers don't stay connected with the country's people."

One of the boys, eager and almost jumping with excitement, asked, "What did you say then, Pooja Ji?" It was as if he expected to be asked the same question in his interview the following year.

Pooja: "I said that they too serve the country, and foreign service officers play a vital role in strengthening India at the international level. However, my preference is to work on developmental projects directly with people. When a person works in their area of interest, they don't have to make extra efforts; their efforts come naturally. So, if I get a position that allows me to work directly with the public, that would be best for me. It matches my personality. However, if I get a different service, I will still strive to give my best and work efficiently and innovatively."

The curiosity of those standing around continued to grow.

Another girl, Jyoti, who was Pooja's friend, asked, "Did they ask you about women's empowerment?"

Pooja: "Of course. How could they miss that? When they see a female candidate, it's all about women—women's education, low sex ratio, the impact of urbanization on women's roles, the role of women in the rural economy, and women's participation in politics. It was all about women. They should have asked me a few questions about men too."

Pintu: Look at this incredible irony; questions about women's empowerment are asked of women, and questions about women's empowerment are also asked of men. Who will discuss issues related to men, brother? Everyone started laughing.

Manoj: Pintu's concern is valid. We hope that questions related to men will be asked in Pintu's interview.

Pintu: They will only be asked if we can reach the interview; we can't even pass the preliminary exam. If we ever reach the interview stage, whether we get selected for the final or not, marriage will definitely happen. No one was particularly interested in what Pintu had to say, and he quickly sensed this. Changing the atmosphere, he said, "Anyway, whatever happens with my interview is a later concern; you tell us how yours went. You gave your interview today; this time, you're the groom of this wedding, Manoj. If I wear a sehra (traditional wedding headgear), these people will start beating me."

Manoj: The board asked me some questions about globalization in the Indian economy, technical innovation, and administrative reforms. Yes, they asked for suggestions to strengthen Panchayati Raj and urban bodies. At one point, it felt like a member of the interview board was really confronting me.

Curious, everyone asked... what happened?

Manoj: They asked me to give a suggestion for the development of democracy in light of Panchayati Raj. I said that with the arrival of Panchayati Raj, people at the village level would be able to vote and choose their representatives. Democracy will reach the grassroots; the people in the Panchayat will be involved in policymaking and implementation, which will undoubtedly create a better system. However, the biggest need is for leadership to be visionary. This means that the more literate and visionary the representatives are, the easier it will be for them to use the administrative framework in the public's interest. Otherwise, when leadership is weak, local administration goes beyond the control of the people, and officials prioritize their interests first and the public's interests later.

Vivek: Then...

Manoj: Then what? They asked the next question: do you think only educated people should become leaders? Shouldn't those who are uneducated have a chance to become representatives? Many people who weren't highly educated have proven to be good leaders.

Then I said, "Sir, being a leader is a quality; it's the ability to unite everyone and take everyone along that defines a leader. It might be that a highly educated person lacks this quality, while an uneducated or less educated person possesses it. However, for active involvement in policy formulation and execution, it's very important for a leader to be visionary. It's not necessary for vision to come only from formal education or degrees. Experience gained from experts, work experience, and understanding the best innovations and practices happening in other Panchayats, cities, and states also contribute to vision. In this globally developing technical world, having a basic level of education is essential for any leader to comprehend these aspects; otherwise, how can vision develop? A leader without vision can create a ruckus for their people, but they cannot provide solutions to their problems.

Such a leader will fall victim to a corrupt, lazy, and negligent system. Therefore, for the better development of Panchayati and local systems, we must create a path for leadership to become visionary." Manoj spoke this entire dialogue in one breath. Everyone present was dumbfounded. They all started clapping vigorously. Pintu stepped forward, hugged Manoj, and said, "This boy can not only become an IAS officer but also a Chief Minister in the future." Everyone burst into laughter.

Another participant came forward: "Manoj brother, your selection is guaranteed; no one can stop you."

Manoj said, laughing, "Until the result is announced, we should not be overconfident. A person should not live in overconfidence like Napoleon. Napoleon attacked Russia in winter. It gets cold in Russia, often dropping to fifty degrees below zero. The result was that Napoleon's army suffered more from the cold than from the Russian soldiers. After consistent victories, Napoleon fell victim to overconfidence, thinking he could attack even in winter. So, we have given our best in our interview; if the circumstances are in our favor, we will surely succeed in this examination."

Manoj, Vivek, and Pooja were happy after the interview went well, and the excitement spread among the other candidates preparing with them.

# Chapter-4

In the preparation for competitive examinations, it often happens that if someone alongside you is continuously succeeding in exams, the likelihood of others succeeding also increases significantly. In competitive examinations, besides studying alone, having a good group is also very essential. I received a lot of support in my preparation from Manoj and Pooja. Manoj has been somewhat of a mentor for us. Vivek was telling this to some boys sitting on the terrace. At that moment, Pintu and Manoj also arrived.

Pintu: Hey brother, when will your results come out? It's been a long time; my throat is dry; let's have a party to celebrate the results!

Manoj: Look brother, this time is not just a new year; this year is 2000, marking the beginning of a new century. The results could also come in a new style. Until then, keep your hopes in check, dear Pintu.

Vivek: Brother Pintu can manage hopes, but not his girlfriend. She has threatened that if he doesn't get selected next time, she will marry the neighbor.

Everyone starts laughing...

Manoj: What, Pintu, is this true?

Pintu: We've also threatened our girlfriend that if she marries someone else, we will marry her friend Priyanka. She has been pursuing us for a long time.

Manoj made a sarcastic remark, but Pintu, how will your selection happen—when you're filling out the form, I say, study hard, and you say, "Dude, there are still six months left. If I study now, I'll forget everything." When there are six days left before the exam, you say, "I haven't studied till now; what can I achieve by studying now?"

Pintu: This is my life's management plan; you petty beings can't understand it.

Manoj: Share your plan; we will definitely understand, so please bless our petty intellect by showing us the right path, Pintu brother.

Pintu: I'm a miserable wretch; whenever I start something, it goes the opposite way. I studied hard for the tenth board exam, thinking I would top. On the day of the exam, the most beautiful girl in the neighborhood was standing on the terrace drying her hair. While looking at her, I was heading to the exam center when I fell into an open manhole. I didn't wake up until six months later when both my leg bones healed. The next year, after some adjustments, I passed tenth, so I said I would take Biology and become a doctor. My family insisted on taking Math to become an engineer because they had to spend money on my education, so I ended up with Math. For two years, Math and I endured each other. In two whole years of intermediate, I scored a maximum of four marks out of a hundred in school internal exams.

If the government hadn't changed in the assembly elections that year and centers weren't set up in schools, I wouldn't have been able to pass intermediate with thirty-four marks in Math. After intermediate, I went for army recruitment, but my height was too short; I went for police recruitment, but my knees were too crooked. I filled the bank exam form, but that year they set the minimum qualifying score to fifty-five percent. I filled the form to become a teacher, but the recruitment was stopped. The girl I liked got married to a doctor in two months, the second girl I liked got married to an inspector in a month and a half, and the third girl I liked got engaged to a company secretary in just a week. There was a commotion among all the girls in the neighborhood; if they want to marry a settled guy, they should hang out with Pintu, and soon the relationship will be secured. Now, when I came here, I step carefully.

All the boys laughed at Pintu's self-deprecating humor.

Vivek: Wow, Pintu brother!

Pintu: Leave me alone; life is a lambda race. I've understood it; I won't fall into its illusion.

Manoj: Lambda, what is that?

Pintu: That is the secret of life, guru; Pintu won't give it for free.

Vivek: So what knowledge will Pintu give?

Pintu: Love; I will give you love.

Manoj: So our love is offered at your feet, Pintu Dev!

Pintu: Not your love, guru; I want the love of all your girlfriends. What use are you all to me?

Everyone started laughing at this.

Manoj: But what is this lambda? Share some wisdom, my friend.

Pintu: You've studied physics; you must have studied it up to the tenth grade. Physics teaches that when a wave travels between two points, the measurement of that wave is done in lambda.

Vivek: But what does this have to do with life?

Pintu - Birth and death are the two points between which all our wave motions are taking place; this wave is our life. Now, whether this wave is big, small, intense, or weak depends on many factors. Some of these factors depend on us, such as hard work and discipline, while some are beyond our control. Those are called external forces. For the wave, these external forces can be the speed of the wind, seasonal temperature, pressure, and the right direction, but in the case of life, these external forces are nothing but fate. Its determination occurs within the wave itself. Internal and external forces together determine the motion of the wave. It is certain that some will have a higher lambda value and some a lower, and all our lives are part of this lambda race. In simple terms, it may happen that despite hard work and discipline, someone's lambda value remains low because their external elements are not in their favor. On the other hand, it is also possible that an average performer's external elements give them better direction and an opportunity to understand the new value of their life, resulting in a lambda value better than others. This is the lambda race, and no one is untouched by it.

After listening to Pintu's lambda theory, everyone fell silent. Manoj and Vivek began to think about what Pintu had said. Some of the boys found Pintu's words to be a bit overwhelming, while others got immersed in their depths. Deep thoughts either bounce off or pull you into their depths. Pintu looked at everyone in astonishment and said, "Hey, you guys won't understand me. That's why I say I am a wretched unfortunate person. Whenever I do something good, it turns out the opposite.."

Suddenly, everyone regained their consciousness. Vivek said, "Pintu bhai, whether you become an officer or not, you will become something great; your lambda is there."

All the boys started laughing again.

Pintu changed the topic and said, "Our lambda is what it is, but pay attention to Roshan's lambda value; that boy's lambda value is bound to deteriorate. You guys should talk to Roshan. Last year, his girlfriend got into the IAS. Since then, the boys have started pulling Roshan's leg, saying, ' now she is out of your reach.' We all took this lightly, and Roshan didn't take it seriously either. But a few days ago, his girlfriend returned from training, and there was a guy with her. People are saying that this boy has been selected for the IPS. Now both of them share a deep friendship. Roshan has stopped talking to the girl. When she came to Delhi, she met all the girls in her hostel but didn't invite Roshan to meet her. Since then, Roshan has been staying locked in his room; it's been ten days, and he hasn't come out nor spoken to anyone. We only see the light turning on and off. We hope we don't hear news one day of something hanging from the ceiling fan."

Upon hearing Pintu's words, the boys said, "What are you saying, Pintu bhai? Speak positively."

Then another voice came from behind, "Hey, Pintu bhai, what about Rajiv?"

Pintu replied, "Oh man, whose case should we discuss? Everyone comes here to become a collector and ends up becoming a lovesick fool. They don't understand biology; only the female chooses the strong male. In simple terms, the whole essence is that successful women cannot love unsuccessful men, even if they end up marrying them out of necessity or mistake. Successful and cunning men prefer unsuccessful women to maintain a happy household.

Unsuccessful women and unsuccessful men live only in the dream of successful love; successful women and successful men are two opposite poles whose union is either impossible or they live in compromise, burning their hearts. There can be exceptions, but I don't talk about them; I speak about the general scenario.

Now, Rajiv loves a girl from his town. He has been in love with her since school. He came here to become an IAS for her. Until now, he hasn't been able to clear the preliminary exam of the UPSC, let alone the mains or interview. His lambda value has reached minus. Meanwhile, the girl's father has fixed her marriage with a computer engineer, and she is going to Hyderabad. We advised Rajiv to tell the girl to convince her family to wait for another year. If he hasn't cleared the IAS by then, he can at least clear the PCS(Provincial civil services) and get married.

Manoj – You're right; these boys preparing for competitive exams will end up losing their sweethearts to engineers, doctors, and MBA graduates.

Pintu – I found out that for the last two years, the girl had been postponing things for her family. This time, the family has pressured her to find out if there's any issue, as she keeps delaying the marriage.

Meanwhile, this guy had given the PCS exam, but there are court cases on those papers. The result of the preliminary exam is still pending, for over a year. The mains and the rest are far away.

Another boy standing there said — Is it necessary to become an IAS or IPS? If government jobs are what matters, there are other recruitments that should be applied for too.

Pintu — Rajiv has already applied for the sub-inspector recruitment twice. Once, the paper was leaked, and for the other time, the result was never declared.

Manoj — Paper leaks are a curse for candidates. In India, getting a job means gaining a new life. In such cases, paper leaks in competitive exams are extremely demoralizing. For many, it is their last chance, and they prepare under tremendous psychological pressure. When a paper leaks or gets canceled, their motivation fades. All their hard work and preparation go down the drain, and they have to dedicate the time allotted for other activities to prepare again. Additionally, due to delays in selection sessions or batches, candidates incur financial losses in their future careers.

Vivek continued from Manoj's point, saying, "Many candidates fall into depression because of this, and it starts affecting their personal lives." Just then, a boy present there remarked that many candidates have the resolution that they will marry, have children, or engage in other activities only after selection. In life, there is a maximum biological age for doing all these things, but the age for getting a job or selection keeps increasing. The vast gap between expectations and results breaks candidates down from within.

Pintu — Just last year, the result of the PCS exam was announced. One boy was crying inconsolably. At first, everyone thought he must not have passed, but when I tried to find out, I learned he had been selected. However, he had been preparing for ten years, and just last month, his father had died after selling the land for his preparation. He was the only son among three sisters. But when the selection of his father's son happened, neither were they alive nor was the land left.

There was another boy who had resolved that he wouldn't return to the village until he got selected. He didn't want to return with a defeated face; his mother was very ill. In the end, his mother passed away, and he was still not selected. Two years after this incident, he was finally selected. There was a boy who was completely sure that a deserving candidate like him would get selected. He was confident based on his performance in all the exams and interviews of the public service commission. The results were declared, and everyone except him got selected. He was devastated, and he hasn't been selected to this day.

A silence fell over the group after hearing this.

No one spoke for a long time...

Then Manoj said, "Look, no one has forced anyone to prepare for these exams. Everyone has come here for some reason and knows that reason well. Everyone knows what will happen if they don't get selected. No one is unaware of this, so instead of being too negative, it's better to do what can be done in our favor. The results can be in our favor, so we should prepare well and move towards our goal. I see that many people are just wasting their time here, so it's no surprise if they don't get results."

As Manoj was speaking, loud screams were heard from the fourth floor of the other building. It was eleven at night, and hearing such wailing screams, the boys rushed towards that direction. All the boys reached the room from which the sounds were coming. At that time, they saw a boy living there was crying helplessly, and another boy from the adjacent room was trying to calm him down. The distressed boy had thrown all his room's belongings around, ripped his books apart, and torn down various maps and posters used for preparation that were stuck on the walls. Everyone who arrived there tried to console the boy, but he was so distraught that he couldn't contain himself and started crying uncontrollably, sitting in a corner.

A little while later, it became clear that he had just come from talking to his girlfriend at the PCO. His girlfriend had said that she no longer wanted to continue their long-distance relationship.

As the boy stepped out of his room, all the boys started discussing among themselves, saying, "Look, we were just talking about this, and it has happened." The boys chatted for a long time, and the conclusion they reached was that students preparing for the IAS-IPS forget thousands of small joys in the pursuit of a big happiness associated with selection, essentially stopping living their lives. In the end, out of a thousand, nine hundred ninety do not get selected, and even the one who does is not guaranteed happiness in life. There remains just one point: he has become an officer, a big shot.

Pintu said, "Hey, prepare well, with all your heart, stay happy, and without any worries; whatever will happen, will happen."

# Chapter 5

It was evening, and the orange hues of the sunset were spreading across the sky. Manoj was standing alone on the terrace where his friends usually gathered at night to chat. Just then, Pooja opened the terrace door and gently placed her hand on Manoj's hands, which were fixed on the setting sun.

Manoj, surprised, said, "When did you arrive?"

Pooja replied, "Just now... What are you thinking about? The results are coming out tomorrow."

Manoj said, "Nothing much."

Pooja said, "Oh, just tell me... I know you don't like to express your feelings, but if you tell me, I'll feel that you have a special place for me in your heart."

Manoj smiled and replied, "Oh, so you want to know your worth..."

Pooja said, "No, I already know that. I just want to know what you were thinking so seriously."

Manoj took a deep breath for a moment...

Manoj said, "Yeah, I'm thinking a bit. This was my last attempt; my father sold land to send me for studies. People in the village used to mock that the son of a grocery store owner would now become a collector. There was a lot of laughter in the family as well, and my father took it to heart. The money meant for my sister's education was spent on me, so she couldn't even come out of the village while I could prepare here in Delhi. I have been here for the past six years. Selection has always been delayed for some reason. My first two attempts were wasted just in clearing the Prelims and Mains. Last time, I missed the final selection by just three marks. This is my fourth and final attempt, so I am a bit anxious. There is a lot of hope and expectation from the family."

Pooja said, "Think positively; something good will happen. Your interview went very well. I'm sure you will make it."

Manoj said, "But I am very happy for you. The hard work you've put in is showing results. Out of thousands, only a few reach the interview stage in their first attempt."

Pooja said, "I can understand your situation; this is my first attempt, and I am nervous about the results too. I pray to God that you get selected so that we can move forward in life. I have seen many dreams for both of us."

Manoj replied, "Pooja, not everyone gets opportunities in this society. Many times, parents can only afford to bet on one child in the family. That bet is nothing but an opportunity, and you have to win it. If you lose, it's not just your loss; the whole family loses, and the chance to move ahead goes away."

Pooja took both of Manoj's hands in hers and said, "Get ready; your destiny is about to change from tomorrow. My heart says you will do something that will make history. But let's put aside these heavy discussions and come on, recite a poem for me..."

Manoj starts laughing, "Why should I recite a poem?"

Pooja said, "You are a Hindi student... you must know some poetry, especially on love."

Manoj replied, "Oh, I'm a poetry thief; I can only recite a poem by some great poet."

Pooja insisted, "No, absolutely not! Those who are in love weave their own poetry... you should weave some for me, for my sake..."

Manoj stood there hesitantly, "Oh, I'm a roadside poet. I don't know how you will like it."

Pooja said, "Whatever you recite will be timeless. Just recite it."

Manoj could no longer refuse...He started reciting some lines of his poem in Hindi.

| | |
|---|---|
| तुम भी क्या<br>एक ही गीत<br>बार-बार सुनती हो<br>प्रेम में आदमी अक्सर ऐसा करता है<br>हवाओं सा चलता है<br>खोता है, भटकता है<br>चादर की सिलवटों सा सरकता है<br>घुप्प कोठरी के ताले सा खुलता है<br>शायद पलकों में पानी से जाल बुनती हो<br>तुम भी क्या<br>एक ही गीत<br>बार-बार सुनती हो<br>दीवारों में लटके चित्र<br>प्रेम में बोलते हैं<br>तकिये सिरहाने की जगह<br>गले लगते हैं<br>घास बादलों सा भरा बिस्तर लगती है<br>और पर्वत चोटियां, ख्वाबों का मैदान<br>अजब पागलपन है<br>हीरा छोड़, कंकड़ बुनती हो तुम भी क्या<br>एक ही गीत<br>बार-बार सुनती हो.... | Do you too,<br>Listen to the same song<br>Again and again?<br>In love, one often does so—<br>Wanders like the wind,<br>Loses himself, drifts astray,<br>Slides like creases on a sheet,<br>Unlocks like the clasp of a darkened room.<br>Perhaps you weave nets of water in your lashes.<br><br>Do you too,<br>Listen to the same song<br>Again and again?<br><br>Pictures hanging on the walls<br>Begin to speak in love,<br>Pillows, instead of resting,<br>Embrace the neck.<br>Grass feels like a cloud-laden bed,<br>And mountain peaks become Fields of dreams.<br><br>What a strange madness this is—<br>Leaving diamonds, you weave pebbles instead.<br>Do you too,<br>Listen to the same song |

| | Again and again? |
|---|---|
| | |

That entire evening, Manoj and Pooja were lost in each other, oblivious to what would happen the next day. It's important to lose oneself in happiness, for a moment of joy can bring smiles for hundreds of days to come.

The next day, outside the UPSC building at Dhaulpur House, participants were bustling around the notice board. The results had been posted, and participants were jostling to see them. A short distance away, Pooja, Manoj, and Vivek stood confused. In those days, online results were not available.

Along with them, other boys and girls had come to check their results. Such enthusiasm is often seen among students preparing for exams, as they eagerly await their friends' results. This enthusiasm stems from both positive and negative reasons. Some come to check their friends' results because if their friend gets selected, it gives them positive energy and focus for their own preparation. They think, if their peer can succeed, why can't they? On the other hand, some come to see the results to gain reassurance; if their friend doesn't get selected, they can console themselves with the thought that despite all the hard work, they too might not succeed.

In a way, checking a peer's result can yield positive outcomes. Thus, there's always a buzz about what the results will be. The final results were posted on the notice board.Just then, Manoj said, "There's such a crowd at the notice board, and results are posted in only two places."Vivek replied, "I'm feeling tense, I think I might get diarrhea."

Manoj joked, "You're already feeling it!"

Vivek replied, "I get diarrhea under pressure!"

Pooja said, "Let's all go check the results together." The three of them held each other's hands and started toward the notice board.

The boys began pulling out their admit cards from their shirt pockets while Pooja took hers out of a small bag. They had all noted each other's roll numbers on their admit cards to match with the results later.

They joined the crowd at the notice board, all eager to check their results. Pooja and Manoj headed toward one notice board, while Vivek went to the one on the other side. Moments later, Vivek jumped out of the crowd and grabbed Pooja's hand, pulling her outside.

"Pooja Shri Prakash, you topped! You got the sixth rank in the All India list!" he exclaimed.

Pooja said, "Are you serious?"

Vivek replied, "Yes! I got the 383rd rank!"

Pooja, in a mix of joy and apprehension, worried that Vivek might be wrong.

Vivek was showing her his admit card with her roll number written on it.

"Look, this is your roll number, right?"

"Congratulations, Vivek!"

"You too!"

They both began to jump for joy, and other boys and girls around them started congratulating them.

"Pooja, where's Manoj?" she asked.

Vivek replied, "He's checking the results. There's a huge crowd; it must be taking time for him."

They became busy again exchanging congratulations.

After a while, the crowd at the notice board thinned out. Manoj stood facing the board with his admit card.

Vivek, Pooja, and their other friends approached him. Vivek gestured to Pooja to support Manoj, who was staring at the notice board. Pooja went beside Manoj and placed her hand on his shoulder. Manoj turned to her with tear-filled eyes and collapsed into her arms, crying uncontrollably.

"It's all over, Pooja, it's all over."

When dreams shatter, a person feels as if everything within them has ended. That day, Manoj felt just that. After so many years of hard work, what was the outcome? Nothing. Following this result, he wouldn't even be able to sit for future IAS exams due to the limit on attempts.

This result made him realize that he didn't possess the level of competence required to be selected in the exam. This thought was gnawing at him from within. But the bigger question was, how can a hardworking person accept that there was a lack of effort on their part? Undoubtedly, effort and competence are two different aspects. However, if he lacked competence, how did many others, who performed even worse, get selected in the final list? Was believing oneself to be competent a delusion and overconfidence, or was it a genuine shortcoming that Manoj could not accept? Whatever it was, Manoj had not only crushed his own hopes but had also failed to fulfill the dreams of his father and family.

The thought was also recurring in Manoj's mind: if this was the result he was going to get, why did he gamble so many years, his father's money, and his sister's future? The expenses incurred in sending him to Delhi were such that his father didn't send his sister, a brilliant student, to continue her education. The sting of all these thoughts tore at his heart that entire night. He could neither express this pain to anyone nor remain quiet about it. A storm was raging within him, and this storm had shattered all his dreams.

When making life decisions, the greatest dilemma is that when a person does not succeed, they are unable to recover the time, effort, and mental struggle invested. Often, people refrain from trying because they think that if they fail, their investment will be completely wasted.

However, upon closer examination, that's not the case; any effort, time, and energy invested toward a goal are never wasted. Even if you don't achieve your goal, the process of trying develops various knowledge and skills that can help you achieve another goal. Everyone knows this, but a person who has faced a significant defeat is not ready to accept it right away. This is because our minds seek immediate compensation, which does not come easily. They must endure the heat of hard work once again.

# Chapter 6

The next day, participants were discussing the civil service exam results at the tea stall. Manoj was there for tea, accompanied by Vivek. The boys were swarming around Vivek to congratulate him.

One boy approached Manoj and said, "You also gave the interview, what happened?"

Manoj replied, "I didn't make it to the finals."

The boy responded, "Well, that's okay." Saying this, he immediately turned towards Vivek. Manoj felt bad about this behavior, but he understood that it was natural after such results. He had seen the same thing in previous years: once the final opportunity to sit for the exam was over, candidates were considered retired, and those with remaining chances looked at them with pity. It was as if they were made to feel that they had failed to achieve what they were sent to create, and now, without that dream, they had lost their youth. This sense of pity could be quite suffocating.

At that moment, another boy approached Vivek and said, "Wow, Vivek, congratulations! You've made history!"

Vivek thanked him and got surrounded by the other boys. Manoj stood there alone with his cup of tea, overhearing two boys whispering behind him.

Boy 1: "Hey, his girlfriend got sixth rank in her first attempt."

Boy 2: "Whose?"

Boy 1: "His, of course."

Boy 2: "he looks like a fool..."

Manoj could hear their whispers clearly. Frustrated, he threw his tea away and left. After a while, Pintu Ji met Manoj. He had come to console him. Pintu Ji mentioned that the result for the Hindi medium had been very poor this time. A capable person like Manoj didn't succeed because his medium was Hindi, whereas Vivek and Pooja were in the English medium and easily made it through. Both had prepared notes on various topics with Manoj's guidance. It was a great injustice. The ongoing lecture about the injustice faced by students from regional languages in the country continued.

Manoj listened quietly, not wanting to respond. Then someone expressed concern about how students from rural backgrounds and small towns would become IAS-IPS officers when the number of candidates taking exams in regional languages was so limited among successful candidates.

An English-medium student countered that when IAS-IPS officers have to represent themselves on national and international platforms, how can they say they don't know English and only speak Hindi? What would they do if posted in non-Hindi speaking states? What would they do if they got posted abroad? How long would they keep complaining about Hindi?

Pintu Ji immediately replied that if there was a need to learn English during postings, it could be learned then, and training could be provided to selected officers. Selected officers in the Indian Foreign Service have to learn other languages, so they will, but why make it a necessity now?

Then the boy quickly responded to Pintu's comment, saying that if they had to learn English eventually, why not start now? Learning it earlier would increase their chances of selection, and they would have more study materials and books available. This might improve their writing skills, enabling them to demonstrate the administrative efficiency that the examiners expect in their answers.

Upon hearing this, Pintu's face turned red, and he spat out the gutka he had been chewing for three hours, saying that the low success rate of students from regional languages in the civil service exam was unfortunate. However, it was even more tragic that a student from the Hindi medium, once he learns to converse in English, would disdainfully look down upon other students from the same medium.

These English-speaking individuals want candidates who speak Hindi, Tamil, Marathi, Telugu, Kannada, and other regional languages to remain mere laborers and farmers, while they become the lords who create national policies. English creates a kind of intellectual elitism; one must break away from this feudal mentality, and these signs are already appearing in you. Even if you are selected in the future, you will not serve common citizens but will behave like an elite, big gun. Know this fact, knowledge of language may be necessary for this exam, but elitism is not.

Meanwhile, Manoj, caught in this back-and-forth, felt increasingly stifled, sitting silently. He often felt like he should just leave, but every time he attempted to get up, Pintu held his hand to keep him there. Manoj felt as though taking the exam in Hindi had become a curse for him. However, what had happened was now done, and he was trying to come to terms with this fact. No false reassurance could mitigate the loss of not succeeding in the exam.

On the other hand, Pintu was worried about Manoj's troubled state due to the results. He felt it was essential to keep someone with him and not leave him alone. But for Manoj, this was becoming even more suffocating. Often, people can overcome their grief by themselves; Manoj wished for the same, but he was not getting a chance for self-reflection. Pintu's well-meaning interventions were becoming a problem.

That evening, Manoj sat on the parapet of the building's terrace, lost in the sky. Suddenly, he noticed two or three boys coming onto the terrace from below. They didn't see that Manoj was sitting above. The boys were talking among themselves. They were the same boys who used to seek free advice from Manoj on strategies and notes for success in the exam.

Boy 1: "Man, nobody expected Pooja to get such a high rank in her first attempt."

Boy 2: "I feel sorry for Manoj. He got out after the interview in his fourth attempt. His girlfriend got through in her first attempt. Now she'll kick him to the curb in a few days after the training."

Boy 3: "Hey, remember last year's results? Shalu got the twenty-third rank, and her boyfriend Alok was here; once she got selected, she kicked him out of her life first. When she returned from training, a friend of hers came, an IPS officer... stylish, handsome..."

Boy 1: "There's a huge difference in their statuses. Now she'll be in a different class, while Manoj will be in a completely separate class. She'll be associating with IAS and IPS officers, while this guy will just hang around."

Just then, Manoj jumped down from the parapet onto the terrace, startling the three boys. Seeing Manoj's expression, they thought he was going to confront them, as he had overheard everything they said.

Boy 1: "Hey Manoj, we were just..."

Manoj glanced at them and quietly walked down the stairs. Distressed by the negative reactions around him, he returned to his room, lay down on his bed, and then heard a knock at the door. When he opened it, he saw two or three boys had come.

Boy: "Is Vivek here?"

Manoj: "Vivek isn't here; he went out to meet some friends."

Boy: "Manoj, why are you sitting alone and looking so glum?"

Manoj: "What can I do? I'm frustrated; I failed in my final attempt. I have no idea what I'll do in life ahead. Should I perform a mujra for you guys?"

Boys: "Hey man, why are you getting angry?"

Manoj, irritated, stepped out of the room and was going down the stairs when he heard the landlord calling him from behind.

Landlord: "Hey Manoj, there's a phone call for you from your village!"

At that time, it was the era of basic phones, and calls from Manoj's village came to the landlord's house. That day too, the call had come to the landlord's house.

Manoj: "Yes, Uncle, I'm coming."

When Manoj picked up the phone, he learned that his sister had called him. His father was very ill, and he was asked to return immediately. His father had suffered a brain hemorrhage and had a stroke. Hearing this, Manoj was taken aback, and the phone receiver slipped from his hand.

# Chapter 7

New Delhi Railway Station was bustling with people. Manoj was standing in a long queue to board the general compartment of the train that would take him to his village. The line had been organized by the GRP (Government Railway Police) and RPF (Railway Protection Force). Manoj had no choice but to stand in the queue as he couldn't secure a confirmed sleeper ticket due to the sudden urgency to return home. Someone had advised him that while the general compartment would be overcrowded, slipping a ₹50 note to one of the policemen would make it easier to board the train. Once inside, he could find a spot and quietly travel to his destination. With his father seriously ill, Manoj didn't have many options.

Meanwhile, Pooja was rushing down the station stairs toward the platform, frantically searching for Manoj. Vivek was with her. Manoj spotted them and quickly tried to hide his face with his bag while standing in the queue, hoping they wouldn't notice him. A few moments later, he peeked out and saw that Pooja and Vivek had left. Relieved, he resumed waiting for his turn in line.

Suddenly, a hand grabbed Manoj's arm from behind. He turned to see that it was Pooja. Pooja asked Manoj, "What happened that you decided to leave without even telling us?"

Manoj replied, "Father had a brain hemorrhage, maybe even paralysis. I got a call from home, so I'm heading there." Pooja, shocked, said, "Oh, so that's the reason. You could have at least informed us! You didn't tell anyone, just grabbed your bag and left. We were worried... we even thought—" She trailed off.

Manoj interrupted, "You thought I was going to do something drastic because of my results, didn't you?" Vivek chimed in, "No, that's not what we were thinking."

Pooja quickly responded, "Alright, forget all that. If your father is unwell, it's good that you're going home. Just let us know about the situation once you're there."

Manoj hesitated and replied, "I don't think I'll call..."Pooja insisted, "Take your time and call when you feel like it."

Manoj finally said, "I may never call..." Pooja was taken aback. "What do you mean by that?"

Before Manoj could reply, someone in the queue behind him shouted, "Move forward or get out of the line! If you want to chat, do it elsewhere. We're struggling for seats here."

Vivek stepped in to defuse the situation. "Manoj, go talk to Pooja. I'll hold your place in the line." Manoj moved aside, and Vivek took his spot, but people in the queue began complaining.

Vivek reassured them, "He'll be back shortly. I'm not cutting in; I'm just holding his spot."

A few moments later, Manoj and Pooja stood face to face. Pooja asked, "What were you trying to say earlier?"

Manoj replied, "You need to focus on your own life now." Confused, Pooja asked, "What do you mean by that?"

Manoj explained, "I'm going back to the village and may never return."

Pooja was stunned. "And what about me?"

Manoj said, "You should start a new life with new people and new dreams."

Furious, Pooja retorted, "What nonsense are you talking about? What has happened that you're saying all this? You failed one exam, and suddenly, you've given up on everything? You're weaker than I thought!"

Manoj sighed. "Pooja, understand this. If I stay with you, I'll only become a burden on you—a responsibility you didn't ask for."

Pooja angrily replied, "How do you know that? You decided all this on your own without thinking of me! One failure, and you're ready to give up on life? The dreams we shared—are they meaningless to you now? Fine, leave now. I'll endure it, but if you betray me later, it might be unbearable."

Manoj remained silent and began walking back to the queue.

Pooja, overwhelmed with emotion, stepped in front of him, pleading like a lover desperate to hold onto her dreams. "Manoj, please don't do this. I understand your father is unwell, and you must go, but don't say we should separate. Without you, all my dreams will remain unfulfilled. Take your time, deal with your stress, but don't end this!"

Manoj gently held Pooja and said, "Pooja, I shared those dreams too, but now they're all shattered. I feel suffocated here, and if I stay any longer, I might break entirely. Move forward with your dreams. I'll be happy seeing you succeed, even if I'm not part of it."

Tears streaming, Pooja replied, "But nothing matters to me without you. Those dreams will mean nothing."

Manoj said, "Love isn't just about staying together. It's about letting the person you love soar freely, to chase their dreams. I feel like I'm holding you back. I can't live with the guilt of being the reason for your setbacks or blaming you if I fail."

Pooja, hurt and confused, responded, "You're talking nonsense. Start fresh. You've taken physical education diploma; you can pursue that. Life offers many chances. If one door closes, another opens. You should try State PCS exams if IAS didn't work out, or do something else you're passionate about. I'll always support you."

Manoj, resolute, replied, "If you truly love me, let me go. I need to find a better path for myself. Right now, I'm not in a position to promise anything or accomplish much. Let me handle my circumstances and focus on my family. Maybe in time, things will change for both of us."

Pooja stood speechless, her heart heavy with the thought that Manoj didn't trust her devotion. Her love had no conditions or expectations, but this doubt broke her spirit. She decided to speak one last time.

"Fine, Manoj. If someone starts believing that love makes them lose everything, they'll eventually lose love too."

With that, Pooja turned away, tears streaming down her face. Manoj wanted to stop her, to hug her and assure her she would always be in his heart. But fear and uncertainty held him back. Helpless, Manoj returned to the queue.

Vivek asked, "Did you talk to Pooja?"

Manoj replied, "Yes."

Thinking everything was resolved, Vivek said, "Alright, let me know when you're back from the village." As Vivek left, Manoj glanced at Pooja walking away. His heart sank, but he chose to stay silent. Each went their separate ways, carrying the weight of unspoken feelings.

# Chapter 8

The songs of pain resonate in the ears upon separation. Such songs echoed in the hearts of Pooja and Manoj as they parted ways. Both were heading towards their new paths. In the suffocating crowd of the general coach of the train, Manoj could hardly find space on the floor, and the clattering sounds of the train tracks transformed into a music filled with sorrow. Meanwhile, Pooja, sitting in an auto on her way back to her room, also heard that music of sorrow amidst the traffic noise and honking.

When sorrow reaches its peak, a person can lose themselves even in the most melancholic sounds.

Manoj tried hard to hide the tears welling up in his eyes. Society dictates that boys crying are a sign of weakness; they are considered weak, cowardly, and defeated. Manoj placed the bag he held in his lap onto his seat and, while stepping over other passengers sitting on the floor, made his way to the bathroom of the train coach. The bathroom was also crowded with passengers, but upon seeing him, some people stepped out for a moment.

Inside the bathroom, Manoj looked at himself in the mirror. His hair was long, and his beard was unkempt. His eyes were tearful, and after that, he washed his face with water and, after composing himself, opened the bathroom door and headed back to his seat.

As he crossed over the passengers sitting on the floor, he returned to his spot, picked up his bag, and sat down again. He hugged the bag to his chest and rested his head on it, closing his eyes.

On the other side, Pooja sat sadly in her hostel room. Despite the joy of passing her IAS exam, she felt unhappy. Some family members had come from home, and among her friends, she was trying to put on a facade of false happiness. Journalists and news channels were coming to interview her. Various colleges, universities, and institutions were inviting her as a chief guest. Many coaching centers and educational institutions were contacting her to honor her. Within a day, Pooja had become a significant figure, and now every word she spoke carried weight. Their lives had moved in entirely different directions.

The next day, Manoj reached the village station. His friend Chandan had come to pick him up. Upon arriving, the harsh reality hit him that his father had passed away, and people were waiting for him. This news was utterly devastating for Manoj; he crumbled inside. In the village, Manoj's father lived with his only sister, Anju. They had sold a small piece of land to finance Manoj's IAS preparations so he could study in Delhi. Due to a lack of a steady income, they were in significant debt, which Manoj now had to repay, as most of it was incurred during his studies in Delhi. Manoj's mother had passed away ten years ago. His father had opened a small grocery store in the village to sustain himself and Anju. They lived paycheck to paycheck, but during Manoj's preparations, his father never let him feel their hardships.

There was only a two-year age gap between Manoj and Anju, so she was also quite young. After their father's passing, Anju became Manoj's greatest responsibility. For the first time, Manoj realized that when someone close leaves for good, there are so many societal rituals that you can't even mourn properly or think about the fact that your loved one has departed.

As the rituals came to an end, memories flooded back—their room, his father's clothes, and belongings became nails of remembrance, pricking every day and deepening the wounds. After the rituals were completed, the big question for Manoj was how to move forward with life. Anju informed him that their father had been ill for a long time but had kept quiet to ensure Manoj's studies weren't disrupted. He had suffered a heart attack two years ago, and the treatment had incurred substantial debt. That night, as Manoj lay in bed thinking about his father, he realized that death doesn't come from outside; it grows inside us from the moment of birth and emerges at the right time. Before it emerges, one must accomplish something; otherwise, it all ends. The critical question for Manoj was what he would do next. Some people in life are like walls; when they go away, you realize how safe you were because of them. While they are alive, their significance often goes unrecognized.

Manoj's father had a close friend, Sudarshan Prasad, who had been friends with him since childhood. One day, he visited Manoj's home to meet him.

Sudarshan Uncle: "Son, your father's health deteriorated significantly; he passed away before we could get him to the hospital." Manoj: "Oh, Uncle, you helped so much; isn't that enough? If you hadn't been there, Anju would have been left alone."

Uncle: "So, son, what are your plans now? Are you going to go back to Delhi and take Anju with you?"

Manoj: "Uncle, I won't be going back to Delhi. I will stay here. Delhi is an expensive city; I don't have any connections there to find work immediately, and if I go alone, who will look after Anju here? You are aware of our financial situation; I have calculated it, and we have a debt of one and a half lakh. Father invested all his savings in my education, so there is no savings left. All we have now is this two-room house and this small grocery store.

If I make the wrong decision, we could lose everything and face starvation. Whatever I do next, it has to be very well thought out. I can't afford to take any risks anymore,Uncle."

Sudarshan Uncle: "You make a valid point, son; when conditions are unfavorable, one should wait for the right time. No doctor can surpass time; it heals every wound. But what about your studies for the collector's exam?"

Manoj: "I didn't pass that exam. I've had four chances, and I failed each time. In the last attempt, I didn't even make it pass the interview.

Now, there are no more opportunities for that; I will try for other government jobs. All those take time."

Sudarshan Uncle: "That's very challenging now; your father dreamed of you becoming a collector, and you worked so hard!" Manoj: "Success feels like it's always an inch away; failure never allows you to become a hero. I have failed to fulfill my father's dream, Uncle. I have no option but to regret it now."

Uncle: "There's no need for regret; you tried. But what will you do now?"

Manoj: "I will look after my father's shop. In the meantime, I will continue to take exams for other government jobs."

Sudarshan Uncle: "That's fine, but there's no guarantee that you will get a job..."

Manoj: "Uncle, there's no guarantee. I spent eight years preparing for the IAS; I never imagined I'd have to return at the final stage. I'm not thinking of the future now; I'm just doing what I can." Sudarshan Uncle agreed with Manoj's thoughts. Then Manoj asked him, "Okay, Uncle, my father had discussed Anju's marriage with Shyam Prasad Tiwari's son. What happened regarding that? If Anju gets married, it will relieve me of a huge responsibility."

Sudarshan Uncle: "Why don't you go and talk to them yourself?" Manoj agreed to this and requested Sudarshan Uncle to go with him one day to talk to Shyam Prasad Tiwari about it.

# Chapter 9

The next day, Manoj went to Shyam Prasad's house in Patkapur village with Sudarshan Chacha and Chandan to see a match for Anju. Manoj wanted to meet Shyam Prasad and talk to him; he hoped that if Anju's marriage materialized, it would relieve him of a significant responsibility. Another important point was that Anju had liked Shyam Prasad's son for a long time, which Manoj was aware of, so he wanted his sister to marry the boy she liked. A few years ago, Anju's father had initiated talks about her marriage with Shyam Prasad, but at that time, their son was going abroad to pursue a diploma in civil engineering, so they had declined for the time being, assuring that this relationship could happen in the future.

When they arrived at Shyam Prasad's house, the conversation began.

Shyam Prasad: "Look, brother, I spoke with your father about your sister. But nothing was finalized at that time, as Mohan was pursuing his polytechnic."

Manoj: "Yes, I know that, which is why we are here today to take things forward."

Shyam Prasad: "But the circumstances have changed now—both for us and for you. Mohan is now a junior engineer in the electricity department. Many proposals are coming in. Just yesterday, we received an offer of eight lakhs in cash and a car. But we refused."

Hearing this, Manoj and Chandan were a bit taken aback, and Shyam Prasad could see their expressions.

Then Shyam Prasad added: "But we are completely against dowry." Upon hearing this, Manoj and Chandan's faces lit up.

Shyam Prasad continued: "But society is very corrupt; even after having a government job, if a boy doesn't take dowry, people say there's something wrong with him or that he's involved with someone else."

By saying this, Shyam Prasad sought agreement from Manoj and his uncle. Manoj, though reluctant, nodded in agreement.

Shyam Prasad: "But our son is not the type to get involved with girls. He is completely pure; he has only focused on his studies, which is why he is successful."

Everyone was confused about what Shyam Prasad wanted. Manoj said, "Whatever you want, we will make sure to serve and honor you; there won't be any shortcomings."

Shyam Prasad: "Oh son, we don't want anything for ourselves; whatever you give will be for your sister and her household. What do we need? Our lives are over. Our kids are settled; isn't that enough?"

Manoj: "Yes, that's great, so let's discuss moving forward with the proposal."

Upon hearing this, Shyam Prasad called out to his wife.

Shyam Prasad: "Hey, are you listening? How much did the proposal from Malkganj offer for our son?"

Wife: "Eight lakhs, one car, along with household items and five tolas of gold jewelry..."

Shyam Prasad: "Look, brother, we have daughters too, so we have a lot of respect for the girl's family. If we can manage this much, consider the proposal settled."

Manoj was feeling terrible inside. Uncle Sudarshan spoke up to handle the situation: "Shyam Prasad, please give them a chance to think."

Shyam Prasad: "You have the full chance; we have had a relationship with your father for years. But please don't take so long that the opportunity slips away. You know what they say, this offer is for a limited time," and saying this, Shyam Prasad started laughing.

Manoj was taken aback and said, "Yes, absolutely."

Everyone started to have tea, and as soon as Manoj raised the cup to his lips, Shyam Prasad said: "Your father also mentioned that you went to take the collector's exam; he praised you a lot, saying my son will surely become a collector one day, just wait and see what pomp he will have. What happened with that?"

Manoj's face fell silent; he didn't know how to respond to Shyam Prasad, as he knew society doesn't respect struggles until results are achieved.

Later that night, Shyam Prasad was standing on the roof of his large house with his wife. Below, Chandan was riding his old Yamaha bike with Manoj and Uncle, heading home; they had all arrived on the same motorcycle. There were two big cars were parked outside Shyam Prasad's house, one car had a government board saying—Junior Engineer, Electricity Department. However, Chandan's motorcycle wouldn't start, so Manoj asked him why it wasn't starting.

Chandan: "Oh man, it happens sometimes."

Manoj: "You should have brought a good vehicle, Chandan; we'll lose our dignity in front of the girl's family."

Chandan: "What could we have done? We could have booked a four-wheeler for two thousand rupees; where would we get the money from?"

Manoj smiled by looking up at Shyam Prasad and said, "It will be fine; Chandan knows how to fix it." Shyam Prasad spoke from above: "It would be good if it starts; otherwise, there will be problems tonight."

Hearing this, Uncle Sudarshan quietly remarked, "This man wouldn't even drop us to the village in his car if our vehicle broke down." Then

Chandan said to Manoj, "Dude, it's not starting with a kick—push it, and I'll start it by releasing the clutch in gear." Manoj pushed the bike, and it started. As soon as it started, Chandan, Uncle Sudarshan, and Manoj got on it and left.

Seeing the three of them on the same bike, Shyam Prasad looked at Manoj from the roof and said to his wife, "He wanted to become a collector; all his arrogance is gone now. His father had arrogance also, now it all shattered."

Wife: "Then why were you bothering with him so much?"

Shyam Prasad: "Sometimes, you have to show people their place, and after making them aware of their status, you should push such people away. His father was very arrogant; he ran a grocery store but talked about becoming a collector. Now he'll know his status; the father is dead, and the son is on the street."

Meanwhile, Manoj was unhappy on the bike. He told Chandan, "this motorcycle breaking down was very embarrassing. We made a big mistake coming here as three people. Shyam Prasad assesses a person's status from their minor issues. He wants to be cozy while enjoying the perks, wants to take dowry, but doesn't want to seem greedy for it. When there are so many big proposals lined up, talking about my Anju seems futile, and I've made such a negative impression that everything has turned negative."

Just then, Chandan said, "There won't be a match for Anju here; this man is demanding too much; he's a robber."

Uncle Sudarshan: "Son, the proposal was good, but what can we say now? Your father's time, this man's talks were different, and today they are entirely different."

Manoj: "Many values influence a person's life simultaneously. These values can be of truth or vice, but market values strengthen both of these values more deeply. The honesty of a rich and prosperous person is respected, while the honesty of a poor person is ignored and goes unnoticed. The dishonesty of a rich and prosperous person is considered a business risk, while that of a poor person is a crime. Therefore, market values cannot be denied. This man's son's market value has increased, Uncle; earlier, that value was nonexistent. Now they are in a position to reclaim that value. In such a scenario, it's less likely that they will agree to Anju's proposal. Anyway, it seems like problems are coming at me from all sides in life. It feels like God is angry and wants to ruin me."

Sudershan uncle - Many times in life, what happens to you today may only make sense years later, and then you feel that what happened was indeed right.

The motorcycle was moving steadily towards the village with a rhythmic "ghud-ghud" sound. As soon as they reached the village, Chandan parked the motorcycle in the courtyard of Chachaji's house. At that moment, a thought crossed Sudershan Chacha's mind, and he felt he should share this with Manoj.

Sudershan: "By the way, there's another proposal; there's a relationship elsewhere. The boy is a clerk. Shall we think for this proposal for anju?

Manoj started to think. Just then, Chandan interjected, "But the boy has a government job; there would be complications too."

Chachaji replied, "There will be difficulties, but the problem is different; there's no dowry."

Manoj: "What do you mean?"

Chachaji: "The boy's father has a condition that he will marry off his son only after his elder sister's marriage."

Manoj: "So what's the problem? We can wait until the boy's sister gets married."

Sudershan: "The elder daughter was married once; within ten days of the wedding, the groom died in an accident. Since then, people have spread rumors that the girl is inauspicious. No one is daring to marry her. She has been living at her father's house for the past six years, and they say they won't marry off their son without the girl being remarried."

Manoj listened to Sudershan Chacha's words and thought for a while.

And then he said, "Okay, I understand, but for now, I will try for the match for Shyam Prasad's son. I will mediate with one or two more people to see." With that thought, Manoj went inside the house.

# Chapter 10

Generally, people have two types of egos. The first type is a superficial ego that arises from good looks, a good job, a strong body, status, family prestige, and success... This is a straightforward ego that brings aloofness, rudeness, and arrogance in people. Because this type of ego is very common, it can happen to anyone, even to insignificant people. Ego is just ego...

The second type of ego is classic; not everyone has it, only the humble and cunning ones possess it. When you compliment a person's beauty, job, status, prestige, or success, they express gratitude and say thank you. But if you praise someone else's beauty, job, status, prestige, or success in front of them, then you become their target, and they will remind you of the big mistake you've made. That person cannot get out of their self-obsession. The ego of a humble person cuts straight to the root without humiliating them. Shyam Prasad was a vivid example of this classic ego.

Four months had passed regarding Shyam Prasad's son's marriage. Manoj had contacted through several mediators for the relationship, but Shyam Prasad was very shrewd, neither rejecting nor accepting the proposal. He was just wasting Manoj's time like a pendulum. At times, he had even pointed out how Manoj could propose the relationship. However, when face-to-face, he would give signals to continue the conversation about the relationship politely. It seemed they were not ready for the relationship between their son and Anju, and Manoj felt that if he could fulfill Shyam Prasad's hidden dowry demands, Anju could marry the boy of her choice. Therefore, in the meantime, Manoj had reopened his father's grocery store and was trying to manage his and Anju's expenses with the small earnings from that store.

That night, while having dinner, Manoj told Anju that he wanted to go to Delhi for a few days. He had some friends there who were now in good positions. They might be able to help him and Anju get out of this predicament.

Anju agreed and said she could manage the house and store for a week without any problem. Manoj was thinking of meeting Pooja and updating her about his situation. Based on the respect Pooja had for him, he hoped she could help him somehow. He planned to request Pooja to take some leave and come back to the village with him. If Pooja accompanied him to Shyam Prasad's place, her IAS position would likely prevent Shyam Prasad from saying no, or perhaps Pooja would suggest another way.

Manoj was confident that due to Anju's future sister-in-law, Pooja would certainly be able to do something. Manoj told Sudershan Chacha that Anju would be alone for the next four days while he completed an important task and returned from Delhi.

The very next day, Manoj reached Delhi.

In Delhi, Manoj first went to Pintu's place. Pintu was surrounded by boys at the tea stall, as usual, recounting his selection tales, explaining how life magically changes after getting selected. The boys were caught in his web, as always.

Seeing Manoj arrive, Pintu immediately jumped up, pretending to remember he had left his purse in the room.

The boys said, "No need, Bhaiya, we'll pay." Pintu insisted that, as the elder brother, he should treat them to tea. All the new boys were enchanted by his generosity and warmth. Manoj smiled at the spectacle.

Seeing Manoj getting closer, Pintu told the boys, "Alright, brothers, let's go..."

All the boys greeted Pintu warmly. By then, Manoj had arrived. Pintu hugged him.

As soon as Manoj arrived, he asked the first question: "Is the wind of bragging still blowing, Pintu?"

With a smile, Pintu replied, "It's the same old formula, life is lambda, my friend... Every year a new batch, new boys, new dreams, new stories... Everyone needs a hero in their stories. I create the hero in their story. Am I doing something wrong?"

Manoj burst into laughter and said, "People are so distressed and sorrowful that you could sell them courage, Pintu. This could open up a career option for you tomorrow: Pintu, the International Motivational Speaker... Heal the heart's pain with three sessions for just two hundred rupees, keep dreams alive with five sessions for only four hundred rupees."

Hearing this, both burst into laughter.

After a while, both were in Pintu's room. Manoj inquired about Pooja and Vivek, and he learned that both had started their training. Vivek was training in Faridabad, while Pooja had gone to Almora for IAS training. Manoj was curious to know what happened to Pooja after he left Delhi. Pintu told him that a few days after Manoj's departure, Pooja had also left Delhi for her hometown, Pune.

Pintu informed Manoj that some state civil service vacancies were coming up, and he should fill out the form.

Manoj replied, "I will fill out the form, brother, but right now I want to stabilize my situation and, first of all, get my sister married. Once the wedding happens, I will prepare and may even return to Delhi to teach for pocket money while studying."

Pintu asked, "What will you do with the shop in the village after your sister's wedding?"

Manoj said, "We will close that shop, and after my sister's marriage, there won't be any compulsion to stay in the village. The results of government jobs can take a year, two years, or even three years. Why should my sister suffer because of me? The entire family has been distressed due to my education. My father is no longer in this world."

Pintu nodded in agreement and asked why he had come to Delhi. Manoj then shared all his plans with Pintu.

Pintu suggested that before going to meet Pooja, he should go to Faridabad to meet Vivek; perhaps he could get a phone number for Pooja's training center. It would be better to call Pooja in advance before going to Mussoorie. Pooja might even be coming to Delhi. At the very least, Manoj should get information about where Pooja was from Vivek.

Manoj liked Pintu's idea. At that time, Vivek was undergoing for training at the National Academy of Customs in Faridabad. Since Faridabad was close to Delhi, the next day Manoj went to meet Vivek.

After chatting for a while, when Manoj asked for Pooja's phone number, Vivek provided him with a contact number for Pooja's training center. Mobile phones weren't widely accessible then, and very few people used them.

When Manoj called the training center, he learned that Pooja was on a fifteen-day field project with her batch that would end in two days.

Manoj told Vivek that he had left Anju alone in the village. He couldn't wait that long, so he decided to go to Mussoorie to meet Pooja.

Hearing this, Vivek said, "As you think is appropriate."

A little later, Vivek mentioned to Manoj that it was time for him to go back to his hostel, so Manoj was preparing to leave. Then Vivek said to Manoj:

Vivek: "Manoj, there's something very important I needed to tell you."

Manoj: Yes, go ahead, what is it?

Vivek: Manoj, don't go to meet Pooja.

Manoj: Why, what happened?

Vivek: There's a guy, Ashish, who has been selected as IAS from this batch. His father was the DGP, and his mother is also an IAS officer. He has proposed to Pooja. I didn't want to tell you this, but I thought if you go to Mussoorie, there might be some drama, so I decided to let you know.

For a moment, Manoj felt paralyzed, but he composed himself and said casually, "Oh, I was just going to meet her. I don't intend to interfere in Pooja's personal life. She is such a big officer—intelligent, smart, and beautiful—so surely other guys would want her too."

Vivek: I understand your feelings. If you want, you can talk to Pooja once; she might be able to tell you better. But I thought it was appropriate to inform you. I'm sorry, brother.

Manoj felt like he was swallowing poison. But he didn't let any of this show on his face or demeanor.

Manoj: Vivek, you did the right thing by telling me. I will think about it before going to Mussoorie.

After a while, Vivek left for the hostel. After meeting Vivek, Manoj was lost in thought about what he should do. His mind was telling him that he shouldn't completely trust Vivek's words and that he should definitely meet Pooja to get the truth. But then he thought, maybe Vivek was right; after all, Pooja hasn't tried to contact him even after all this time.

Manoj was caught in a dilemma; he decided he must meet Pooja at least once. His heart was unable to fully trust Vivek's words but couldn't completely dismiss them either. After some time, he arrived at the railway station. At the information window, he came to know that the train to Dehradun was at platform number three, and the train to his village was coming to platform number five. He bought a ticket to Dehradun and boarded that train.

Once again, the inner conflict roared within him: What was he doing? What if he went there and found Pooja in Ashish's arms? Would he be able to accept that? If he couldn't, what could he do? Nothing; he should get off. Then another thought struck him: he had helped Pooja prepare so much that she became an IAS officer. Didn't he have the right to go to her and ask for her help? And what would happen if he abandoned Pooja at this point? Anju's marriage plans would fall apart, and his plan to come back and live in Delhi would also be ruined.

 He would always have to settle for running a grocery store in his village as his future. Pooja couldn't be abandoned like this. Even if she was in a relationship with Ashish, he would convince her to come back with him. And if she refused, he would threaten to tell Ashish about their relationship. If necessary, he would even mention their private moments that might create doubt In Ashish's mind about Pooja.

At that moment, Manoj's mind was flooded with conflicting thoughts. But then a voice from his heart spoke: "Manoj, you've become blinded by your self-interest. Your bad circumstances have made you so cunning that you can't think clearly. You don't want Pooja because she loves you, but now your main reason for wanting her is that if she's with you, Anju's marriage will happen, your future will be secured, she will bear your expenses, and you can prepare for PCS, freeing yourself from the grocery store and village life. You want to connect with Pooja only for your benefit. The girl who used to mean love to you, with whom every moment spent was a reason to live, you are now considering turning those beautiful moments into a spectacle, exposing the privacy of your relationship to ruin her honor."

"Manoj, you know Pooja can lead a better life after becoming an IAS officer, and she should now connect with someone of her stature. You've always known that if your exam result was negative, you would have to make this decision. But now you want to stay connected to Pooja so she can serve as your bank account. Maybe Ashish truly loves her; would you still want to plot against their relationship? If you truly love someone, it's measured by how much you respect them after they leave and how much you value the confidentiality of what has transpired between you."

Just then, the engine of the Dehradun train blew its whistle, and the train began to move slowly along the tracks.

Suddenly, a loud voice echoed in Manoj's mind: "Don't think about all this nonsense. If you think too emotionally, you'll spend your whole life like a dog. Make a plan and win Pooja back. It's easy to get carried away with emotions, and it's hard to swallow the bitter truths of life. Sometimes you have to spit and lick your wounds." Saying this, Manoj sat firmly in the train.

That night, the train rattled along towards its destination, and Manoj sat quietly in his compartment.

# Chapter 11

The next day, Manoj was disembarking from the train at his village platform. Life often offers easy paths that can lead you to comfort and luxury, but in return, it asks for your honest intentions. These honest intentions may not yield immediate benefits and can stick to you like a stale, rotten habit, filling life with the stench of struggle. Most people cannot overcome this stench and get buried in it. This is why most people shake off honest intentions as soon as they get the chance, while those who nurture them retain their spirit even in struggle; it develops within them like a fossil and eventually transforms into a formidable energy, an energy that will either generate electricity or become a diamond. Whatever is produced will shine so brightly that it will illuminate the world.

Last night, Manoj had made a decision in the turmoil of life and had chosen a path for himself. He returned to his village without meeting Pooja.

When Manoj reached home, Anju was eagerly waiting for him. Manoj had nothing to say to Anju, and he didn't know how to explain the decision he had made. Anju simply asked, "What happened, brother?" Manoj replied, "Just give me something to eat..." He was given curd and flattened rice. After a short rest, Manoj felt useless and hopeless since he had not met the people he was hopeful about; now he had no hope of a match for Anju with Shyamaprasad's son.

Anju became sad. Although one-sided, she had a corner in her heart for Shyamaprasad's son, and that corner was now empty. The whole day, the siblings remained silent. Manoj sat in the shop all day, trying to find Anju and his future with his gloomy eyes, but he couldn't make sense of anything. Several times he thought about whether not going to Mussoorie was a foolish decision. But then his heart urged him to stay committed to the decision he had made, insisting that it was the right and moral choice. There are no tricks in love, only dedication, a dedication where love's dignity is placed above one's own worth.

Pooja might have already decided to part ways with him, but he had loved her, and every decision he was making now was based on that dedication. If he compromised that dignity, a criminal would reside in his heart forever, one that no one else might see, but he would meet daily. Therefore, it was not only futile but also sinful to think of tying Pooja to himself for his benefit.

Lost in this turmoil, Sudarshan Chacha arrived. When he asked Manoj about his trip to Delhi, Manoj explained in detail that there were no positive results from the trip. Then Sudarshan Chacha informed Manoj that he had received news that Shyamaprasad had arranged for his son's engagement to a girl from a wealthy family in Gorakhpur, and the wedding is next month. Manoj took a deep breath, realizing that things were slipping out of his hands, and making efforts here would be futile and humiliating.

Manoj asked Sudarshan Chacha about another boy he mentioned, who is a clerk and has no dowry issue.

Chacha Ji: Yes, I had mentioned that. What happened?

Manoj: Chacha Ji, let's try for Anju in that family; maybe a match can be made. Chacha Ji agreed to this but reminded Manoj that the condition of that family was that their daughter is a widow whose husband died in an accident just a week after their marriage. The entire community is saying she is ill-fated, but her father insists that they will not arrange another marriage for their daughter until their son gets married. Sudarshan Chacha wanted to know what Manoj would do about this condition.

Manoj replied, "Sudarshan Chacha, let's first talk to them. I will figure out a way.

# Chapter 12

Five months later, the weather had changed; it was evening, and the dim light was on in Manoj's room. The bed for the wedding night was adorned, with Gudiya sitting on it. Gudiya was the same girl whose brother had been betrothed to Anju. Manoj had accepted the condition set by Gudiya's father that the widow's daughter would remarry first, and only then would his son marry. As a result of this condition, Anju was now bound in marriage to Gudiya's brother, and to fulfill the condition, Manoj had tied the knot with Gudiya. The wedding bed wasn't particularly lavish because there was no one else in Manoj's house. His sister was now at her in-laws', and the few distant female relatives who had come to Manoj's house had also left. Most relatives had distanced themselves from Manoj's marriage because, in their view, he had married a widow, considered inauspicious.

Inside the room, Gudiya sat on the bed while Manoj was organizing some papers at another table.

Manoj: "Let's do this tomorrow; we should go to Chandan and Chachaji's place and meet everyone. Now, whoever is with us is all that we have, so it's good to have their blessings."

Gudiya (speaking softly): "Okay."

Manoj continued working while talking: "The rest we'll tell everything tomorrow morning. After mother passed away, Anju has been taking care of Baba. I just kept studying in Delhi. I returned to the village only after Baba passed away. Now we both have to manage this house together. I've started the shop that Baba had, but there isn't any significant income yet. However, if we arrange a bit more stock, it could run. That's how we'll manage household expenses."

Gudiya looked up at Manoj. He had read the questions hidden in her eyes, but despite that, he didn't want to confront them. After a while, when Manoj looked at Gudiya again, she was already looking at him. Manoj felt flustered.

Manoj: "Do you have something to ask...?"

Gudiya boldly asked, "Why did you marry me?"

Manoj: "Why? Everyone has to marry. I liked alliance with your family and you, so I agreed."

Gudiya: "But did you not know anything about me, or did you just marry us to settle your sister's wedding?"

Manoj remained silent for a moment after hearing this. Gudiya thought he didn't want to respond, but then Manoj stopped what he was doing at the table and turned to Gudiya.

Manoj: "If what happened to you, had happened to me, would I have considered myself inauspicious? Maybe I wouldn't have. In this society, there are many paths closed to women but open to men. Many people wait for a woman to have a stain on her character, and then they take care of the rest. When Sita was abducted by Ravana, Lord Ram didn't even know where she was, whether she was alive or dead, or how she was with Ravana.

At that time, there must have been many who said that searching for Sita was pointless; Ravana's companionship must have tainted her. But despite all this, Sri Ram continued to search for Sita; he could have remarried or given up, but he didn't because somewhere the power of Devi Sita's faith was giving him the strength to keep trying in the face of adversity. In this world, equal faith keeps searching for one another. If your arrival in my life has happened, it is the search of two beliefs.

The strength of your faith must be seeking me, and it is that very strength that today has brought us into a marital relationship. Now, we should move forward in this relationship with complete purity and fidelity; that should be our duty."

Saying this, Manoj moved closer to Gudiya and gently took her hand in his. Three to four days after the wedding, Manoj and Gudiya were reopening their shop. Manoj was stocking up the grocery and ration items in the shop attached to their house, lifting and placing sacks. Gudiya was helping him. It hardly felt like a new bride had come to stay in the house.

Just then, Lakhaniya and Baby arrived, carrying a bundle of wood on their heads. Lakhaniya and Baby were daughters of the Musahars living in the southern part of Manoj's village.

Seeing Gudiya helping Manoj, Lakhaniya and Baby said to him, "What happened, Manoj bhaiya? You brought a bhabhi but didn't introduce us. Everything happened secretly in the village."

Baby stepped forward to greet Gudiya and said, "If you need anything, please let us know," and saying this, both moved ahead, perhaps burdened by the weight of the wood on their heads. Just then, Manoj called out to them.

Manoj: "Hey, girls, wait, you both."

The two girls, carrying their bundles, stopped. Manoj then said to Gudiya:

Manoj: "Listen, go get some sweets from inside... the ones that came from your home."

Gudiya brought out a plate of sweets, which included some boondi laddus, balushahi, and snacks, along with a little wet halwa.

Lakhaniya spread her dupatta to take the sweets when Manoj thought that putting food in her dupatta would dirty it as well.

Manoj: "Hey Lakhaniya, take it in the plate... and return the plate later..."

Lakhaniya hesitated. She thought it would cause untouchability. Knowing Lakhaniya's hesitation, Manoj said, "Oh, take it, I'm saying. Why are you overthinking? If you want to keep the plate, just let me know." Manoj laughed, lightening the mood, and seeing this, Lakhaniya and Baby took the plate, assuring they would return it.

In the meantime, while Manoj was climbing onto his shop to put up a light bulb, a jeep and two bullets pulled up. Seeing the vehicles stop, Lakhaniya and Baby quickly left the place. From the bullet, a guy wearing black glasses and a white kurta-pajama, looking like a goon, got down and came towards Manoj, accompanied by two or three thugs. Manoj tried to look closely at the guy and realized it was Ranveer.

Ranveer sat down on a chair near Manoj and said, "What's up, Manoj? Are you setting up the shop?"

Manoj looked at Ranveer and stepped down.

Manoj: "Hey, brother Ranveer, how are you?"

Ranveer: "I'm fine. I found out about your father, but I couldn't come because I wasn't in the village. I went to the city for a party meeting."

Manoj: "Party meeting..."

Ranveer's sidekick: "Bhaiyaji, he is our party's block in-charge. This time, he is likely to get a ticket for the assembly elections."

Manoj: "Oh wow, you've come a long way, brother."

Ranveer: "But what are you doing? You went to give the IAS exam; has the dream of becoming a collector faded?"

Manoj felt embarrassed by this question from Ranveer but knew he could no longer hide from such questions. Gudiya was listening to everything from behind the shop's door. Manoj managed to respond to Ranveer's question by saying, "Well, it didn't happen for me. Now I will work here in the village."

Ranveer: "Then what was the benefit of so much study? This UPSC exam is like gambling; if you win, you're a king, otherwise you're on the street. We both passed twelfth together; you topped while I barely passed. But back then, I used to think why I couldn't be a topper like you. You topped, and my father scolded me a lot. But in ten years, time has turned around."

Ranveer turned to his thugs and said, "You all know, I used to feel very frustrated seeing Manoj, but today I feel pity. Manoj bhai, if you need any help from us, feel free to ask. We studied together; you have that privilege over us." Manoj knew Ranveer had been envious of him since childhood; he had always been a bully but never received the kind of praise that Manoj got for his intelligence. Ranveer came to settle that score from their childhood. Manoj did not take Ranveer's words to heart and simply replied.

Manoj: "It's great to see you, Ranveer. But I have to head out somewhere now. Let's catch up comfortably another day."

Ranveer sensed that Manoj was annoyed by his words, but he wanted to rub more salt in Manoj's wounds. It is the nature of miscreants to find their peak satisfaction in wickedness.

Ranveer: "Alright, guru, keep meeting; your education might also come in handy for us. And yes, there's a game in the panchayat tomorrow. You were a great player in school; if you feel like it, come to watch. The event is from our side." Speaking to his thugs, Ranveer ordered, "Hey, give him a pamphlet." One of Ranveer's thugs handed Manoj a pamphlet pulled from a bundle. The pamphlet contained Ranveer's photo and information about the panchayat game. After this, Ranveer got into his jeep with an air of authority, and his thugs started their bikes and drove away. Just then, Gudiya stepped out from the back door.

Gudiya: "You talk to everyone with so much despair. It doesn't feel good when someone comes and says nonsense to you and walks away."

Manoj: "Calm down. Those whom time beats, everyone makes fun of them."

Gudiya: "So win over time again... We did not marry a defeated man. When no one was holding our hand, you held it. You are a hero in our eyes, and heroes do not lose to time; they walk with it."

Manoj was touched by Gudiya's words. That night, Gudiya fell asleep, but Manoj couldn't close his eyes. He was reading the pamphlet given by Ranveer in the dim light of the room, thinking with his eyes closed. Gudiya's words kept echoing in Manoj's ears.

Gudiya: "You talk to everyone with so much despair. It doesn't feel good when someone comes and says nonsense to you and walks away."

Lost in thought, Manoj eventually fell into a deep sleep.

# Chapter 13

The excitement in the sports field was at its peak, while Manoj could hear the clattering of the railway tracks in his ears. He was trying to focus on the sound of the tracks, and in the moving train, he could see his own reflection on the bag he was leaning over. The noise of the railway tracks grew louder, so much so that Manoj suddenly opened his eyes and found himself back in the panchayat ground. He had come out of the whirlwind of his memories, and in that one moment, his entire past life passed through him in shivers of recollection.

Before his eyes, Lakhaniya and Baby had completed the final sprint and had won. The final moments were intense. Everyone was astonished by the remarkable performance of Lakhaniya and Baby. All the spectators were extremely excited, teasing the male players. The two winning girls were surrounded by the crowd. It was rare in the history of the panchayat games for girls, who had been included in the competition out of pity, to crown themselves with victory in the games. Manoj couldn't comprehend how this miracle had happened. Every person present was astonished by how both girls had outperformed such formidable runners—girls who had neither food to eat nor clean clothes to wear. Yet, they had achieved this feat in front of everyone's naked eyes, making it impossible for anyone to dismiss it as mere talk.

A few moments later, Lakhaniya and Baby were called to the stage to be honored for winning the race. The crowd of boys was climbing over one another to see the two girls. The situation was such that the organizers had to deploy people with sticks to control the crowd and repeatedly announce from the stage to maintain peace.

Lakhaniya and Baby couldn't comprehend what to do now. They had never experienced anything like this in their lives, where people took them with such enthusiasm. But every winner experiences that they must face their victory for the first time, and this victory rewards them for their past defeats and struggles.

This first victory gives every individual motivation and a new direction in life. For Lakhaniya and Baby, this was their first victory that came with a valuable lesson. When the prize for winning the race— a fridge and cooler—was presented to Lakhaniya and Baby, they were overjoyed; they had never imagined such a day, when they would think of a goal and successfully achieve it. When someone fulfills their dreams for the first time and realizes that dreams can indeed be realized, that's when the real joy of life begins. They move from small dreams to larger ones.

On the other hand, Manoj was filled with excitement and felt that if these two girls could achieve such an extraordinary performance despite their difficult circumstances, then why couldn't he take a second chance in his life? The girls' victory changed a lot for Manoj, and perhaps that's why he was very happy, feeling as if he had been given a second chance to live.

In the settlement of the Musahars, Lakhaniya's father, Hardu Ram, was sitting by his hut. Just then, a boy ran in and entered the hut.

Boy: "Hardu uncle, the whole village crowd is coming with Lakhaniya; it seems like there's some commotion."

Hardu jumped up in surprise and ran out of the hut.

Hardu: "Oh God, what trouble has this girl caused?"

Hardu's cousin, Bhikharam, who was Baby's father, was already standing there. By then, other women, girls, and children from the settlement had arrived, wide-eyed, wondering what was happening and why there was such a crowd coming with Lakhaniya and Baby. Hardu and Bhikharam rushed forward and approached Manoj, who was leading the crowd, with folded hands, asking, "What happened, brother? Did the girls do something wrong?"

Manoj took Hardu's hands and told him, "Uncle, the girls have performed magic; they've done something that will make your chest swell with pride."

Hardu took this as a joke.

Hardu: "What have they done, brother? If they did something wrong, please forgive them. They are just girls."

At that moment, the crowd entered the settlement, celebrating joyfully. Refrigerators and coolers were brought in rickshaws. Lakhaniya and Baby were adorned with garlands. The cooler and refrigerator were being placed in their hut as they got down from the rickshaw. The women and men of the Musahar settlement couldn't comprehend what was happening.

Manoj: Uncle, the girls have defeated the boys in today's race. That's why the villagers are happy and have come to honor them with garlands. This is the reward for their victory. The fridge is for Lakhaniya and the cooler is for Baby.

Bhikharam: Which race, brother?

A boy standing there speaks up, "Hey, there was a race in the panchayat today; boys from nearby villages and panchayats came to compete, and Lakhaniya and Baby defeated everyone."

Bhikharam and Hardu were still in disbelief.

Manoj approached Lakhaniya and Baby and said, "You both didn't let me lose face. Otherwise, I thought I would have to run away, tying my towel at the panchayat ground. But you both ran so well that even those who mocked us had to hide their faces and flee."

Both girls nodded in agreement. They were very happy. Manoj knew that the joy of the first victory is priceless because the first win introduces a person to their personality and makes them aware of their potential. Manoj was also very happy because in times of despair, the success of others can provide courage to oneself. He asked the girls, "Now that the cooler and fridge have arrived, what a joy it will be to drink cold water and enjoy the breeze!"

Both girls burst into laughter and said, "But brother, what will happen to the electricity line? Will Puttan Chacha allow us to take the line from his wire?"

Manoj paused, thinking, "Only Puttan knows about his grace."

Then Lakhaniya spoke, "Everything has happened thanks to you. If you hadn't fought on our behalf, we wouldn't have even gotten a chance to run. So how could we have won the race or received the fridge and cooler?"

Manoj responded, "But tell me one thing, how do you run so well?"

Baby: We run much more than this every day.

Manoj: How?

Lakhaniya: Brother, we go to market every morning to sell vegetables, which is eight kilometers away.

Manoj: What do you mean?

Lakhaniya: We carry the potatoes, tomatoes, and green vegetables of farmers from the village who don't want to go sell them. We set off at four in the morning, running to reach the market early because the first to arrive gets to sell their vegetables on the footpath.

Baby: We walk fast for eight kilometers, and then we run and walk. This way, we cover about 8 to 9 kilometers on foot every day.

Manoj: And how much do you carry on your back?

Baby: It must be around 15 to 20 kilograms.

Manoj: Carrying all that back and forth for eight kilometers is a lot.

Baby: Yes.

Lakhaniya: After selling the vegetables quickly, we come back, do household chores, and then go to collect wood from the forest by the river and take the goats for grazing.

Manoj: You both have a lot of courage.

Both girls started laughing.

Manoj told them that his father always said that a person should be like bamboo. Bamboo spreads its roots underground for many years, and when the roots become strong, it breaks through the earth and grows tall. If you want to achieve something great, you must first strengthen that inner power.

# Chapter 14

That night, Gudia and Manoj were lying on the bed. Seeing Manoj's happiness, Gudia couldn't help but ask, "What's the matter? You seem very happy today; I heard Lakhaniya and Baby did an amazing job in the race."

Manoj: Yes, they created quite a stir today. I learned a very big lesson from life today.

Gudia: What is it?

Manoj: The dream you are chasing may not be meant for you, and your real dream might be waiting for you somewhere else.

Gudia: What do you mean? I don't understand.

Manoj: I have found a new dream now.

Gudia: What is it?

Manoj: I will help children like Lakhaniya and Baby move forward. The true victory in life is not just fulfilling your own dreams but also helping others achieve theirs.

Gudia: This is the first time I am seeing you so happy. Don't let this happiness fade away...

Manoj kept staring at the clock hanging on the wall; sleep had vanished from his eyes. But Gudia had already fallen asleep, snuggled against him. Manoj gently moved Gudia's hand away from his chest and went to the room behind the house. He picked up a box and took out a folder from it. From that folder, he pulled out a certificate, which he examined closely: Bachelor in Physical Education.

Manoj remembered that when Pooja came to drop him off at the railway station, she had taken both of his hands in hers and said, "Get ready; tomorrow your fortune is about to change. My heart tells me that you will do something that will make history. You start anew; you have a course in physical training, and you are interested in it. Do something in that field…"

Manoj returned to that moment and went back to the bedroom with the certificate in hand. He couldn't sleep all night. The sleep had disappeared from his eyes, and new dreams were awakening in them. When dreams awaken, sleep does not come. Perhaps that's why he went to face the rising sun the next morning in the fields. He also decided to start running to stay fit from that day on. That day, he was inspecting the fields, figuring out where he could run in the village—where he could exercise and do other physical activities. The villagers were watching him with curiosity, wondering what he was up to. Whenever Manoj noticed people watching him, he tried to act normal.

He walked among the fields and spoke with the boys and children on the village roads. He was estimating what and how he could accomplish his goals.

Early in the morning, after doing all this, Manoj opened his grocery store and sat there with a bundle of old newspapers. He began cutting out articles, interviews, and writings about athletes to compile a file. As people came to buy groceries, he provided them with those articles as well. Manoj closed his shop early that day and rode his motorcycle to the city to buy plenty of books on physical education, immersing himself in studying various formats of running. In this way, for the next few days, he was deeply engaged in studying physical education books, newspaper articles, and better running techniques.

A few days later, one evening, when he returned and sat in front of his dinner plate, Gudiya curiously asked where he had been disappearing to lately. Manoj replied with a smile that he was just starting to run toward his dreams. But there was a big problem: there was no field or playground in the nearby villages.

Gudiya asked, "So what's the problem? If it's just running, you can run anywhere." Manoj started laughing.

Gudiya then asked, "Can I ask you something? If it's just about running, why did you bring so many books? Can you run by just reading?"

Manoj replied, "Oh no, it's to learn techniques."

Gudiya asked, "Meaning...?"

Manoj explained, "In any sport, there are techniques to understand. I'm studying the experiences, rules, and methods of those athletes so that I can work hard in the right direction."

Gudiya said, "Oh, we thought you just had to run like a bull."

For a whole month, Manoj studied various running techniques and maintained a strong and fit body with updated knowledge. After that, Manoj was sitting with Hardu and Bhikharam in their settlement, and Lakhaniya and Baby were also standing there. Manoj told Hardu and Bhikharam:

"Uncle, these two girls are very strong; let me prepare them for sports. Their hard work will take them far."

Hardu replied, "Manoj bhaiya , we are poor; just surviving is enough for us. That's already a lot for us."

Bhikharam added, "Both girls run all day from morning, and we struggle just to gather two rotis... What will they get from all this jumping around?"

Lakhaniya chimed in from behind, "A fridge, a cooler."

Manoj smiled at her.

Hardu continued, "Next year we have to get them married; we've already started looking for boys."

Baby protested, "Oh no, we won't get caught in that mess by marrying so early."

Hardu teased, "Yeah, you two are big heroines, going to get big jobs... Just shut your mouth."

Manoj said, "Uncle, you don't understand; givea chance to  these girls... I found out that in two months, there will be a district-level running competition. I'll train them for it; if they can't do it, that's the end of the discussion. If they win, we'll see what happens next."

Bhikha and Hardu thought for a moment.

Lakhaniya's voice came from behind, "We are ready, Manoj Bhaiya."

Bhikharam, feeling annoyed, said, "Oh, shut up, you chatterbox."

Facing Manoj, Bhikha added, "All that is fine, but these two won't stop going to the market. Just let us know; if we don't earn, we will starve, and then what will they do with all this?"

Manoj, Lakhaniya, and Baby exchanged glances... because this was truly a significant challenge for them. Manoj was just waiting for a little agreement to take charge. He said, "Alright, instead of practicing in the morning, we'll practice in the evening. These two will have to go to work in the morning." That evening, before sunset, Manoj stood on the ground in the village where there was some space to run, along with Lakhaniya and Baby.

"From today, we will start. I will run with you both; we will run five laps around this field, and then I will explain some running techniques to you. Shall we start? Is that alright?" Both girls nodded in agreement. Manoj said, "Then say Jai Bajrang Bali!"

Both girls shouted, "Jai Bajrang Bali!"

After a little while, the three of them comfortably completed five laps of running. After the run, Manoj taught both girls some stretching exercises and told them that they must do these exercises every day after running. While teaching stretching, he noticed that the girls were doing it incorrectly. He corrected them.

Seeing Manoj and the girls, women working in the nearby fields paused to watch them. Some children and elders were also observing. Manoj and the girls ignored them and continued with their work.

The next day, Manoj brought sports shoes for Lakhaniya and Baby and began handing them out. Manoj looked at both girls' feet; their feet looked so hard that it seemed the flesh had been worn away. It hardly seemed like the feet belonged to girls.

"From today, you both will run in these shoes," said Manoj.

Baby exclaimed joyfully, "Wow, these are beautiful shoes! They are so nice that they will not make our stone-like feet look good."

Manoj said, "The feet that you call stones are actually your greatest strength, and this strength will become your beauty."

Lakhaniya and Baby looked at Manoj. Suddenly, Lakhaniya spoke up, "This red one is mine..."

Then both girls started jumping around in their new shoes. For the first time in their lives, they didn't feel a hard surface under their feet.

"Hey Lakhaniya, the ground feels so soft," Baby said. After that, the two of them started walking a short distance in their shoes and then began to jump with excitement.

"How cushioned it feels!" Baby exclaimed.

Lakhaniya said, "It feels really good."

Since Lakhaniya and Baby got their new shoes, they felt like they could fly across the field. Manoj, full of enthusiasm, took Lakhaniya and Baby to the field and worked on their initial preparations. One day, while people were running in the field in the evening, Ranveer Yadav passed by in his jeep. Seeing them running, he stopped his vehicle to watch. Then, out of curiosity, Ranveer Yadav asked one of his men:

"Hey Bablu, what is this Manoj doing with these girls?"

Bablu replied, "Brother, I saw them running yesterday too... Another fellow said the boy from the Musahar community was telling that he is preparing these two for running."

Ranveer scoffed, "This defeated man is going to teach them how to win in life. What a joke!"

Then Ranveer Yadav drove off.

Meanwhile, unaware of all this, Manoj, Lakhaniya, and Baby continued running together as the sun was setting.

# Chapter 15

That day, a customer was standing at Manoj's shop while he was handing over goods. In the village, some customers tend to chew betel leaves until they get their items. Manoj was collecting the goods requested by that man from different drawers in the shop. Once all the goods were out, as Manoj was about to send off the customer, a sound of utensils falling came from inside the house adjacent to the shop. In the next moment, he heard Gudiya scream... Manoj ran over. He saw that Gudiya was lying unconscious near the hand pump in the house, and a pot of milk had fallen, spilling everywhere.

Manoj picked up Gudiya and splashed some water on her face; after a moment, her eyes opened. He supported her and laid her down on the bed. After a while, when Gudiya's condition stabilized a bit, he hurriedly went to Chandan's house and called out to him loudly. Chandan rushed out in a panic, asking what had happened. Manoj said, "Come on, take out the motorcycle; we need to take Gudiya to the hospital." After a short while, Manoj had reached the hospital with Gudiya on the motorcycle.

At the hospital, the doctor examined her and came out to inform Manoj that he was going to be a father. He also mentioned that the test results showed both the mother and baby were weak. The mother's hemoglobin was very low, and the baby's development was not as it should be.

Manoj asked, "So what should I do, Doctor?"

The doctor replied, "Do a few more tests; if there's anything wrong, we can address it now during the pregnancy."

Manoj took the doctor's note, which listed several tests. Hesitantly, he asked the doctor, "How much will this cost?"

The doctor replied, "Look, there aren't any pathology labs nearby. You'll have to go to the city for these tests. It will probably cost around 3-4 thousand."

Manoj stepped outside and left for home with Gudiya, who was sitting outside.

Meanwhile, Ranveer had reached the Musahar colony, accompanied by his cronies. Ranveer sat on a chair, and Hardu, Bhika, and other people stood around, listening to him.

Ranveer asked Hardu, "Has your girl stopped selling vegetables?"

Hardu replied, "No, sahab."

Ranveer continued, "I saw her hopping around with the upper caste people yesterday..."

Hardu explained, "sahab, she is preparing for a race."

Ranveer scoffed, "Now she's going to hop with big shots? Then you'll come crying to me about losing your honor."

Bhikaram interjected, "Did something go wrong, boss?"

Ranveer answered, "Nothing has happened yet, but something will go wrong, and then you'll wake up."

"Until yesterday, you were crying about having no employment. After much effort, I arranged a spot for you in the market, ensuring you could sell vegetables without being harassed. And now you're acting like you're above it all."

Bhikaram spoke up, "... girls are going to sell vegetables every day. They return from the market and then go to practice."

Hardu said, "We thought maybe they'd do well in sports, so we didn't stop them. If you say so, we'll stop them from going."

Lakhaniya, standing behind, chimed in, "Why would they want to stop us..."

Hardu felt the situation was getting out of hand, so he quickly intervened, "Hey, be quiet..."

Ranveer retorted, "Why should she be quiet? She's right... she'll run and run, become a star athlete... but let's hope she doesn't run away completely."

Ranveer's cronies began to laugh. Hardu, Bhika, and the others fell silent, realizing the conversation was spiraling.

Ranveer continued, "Anyway, we've come to help you out. You know Shiva from the flour mill, right?"

Hardu nodded in agreement, "Yes, we know him, brother."

Ranveer informed them, "His daughter and son-in-law have come for a month. They need two girls to take care of their small child and help with work."

Hardu said, "We can send someone, brother..."

Ranveer replied, "Listen, I've already named these two girls. If they fit the bill, you can send them to work starting tomorrow. They'll get a hundred rupees a day, and if the couple likes them, they might take them back to the city with them. Then they can earn a monthly salary."

Hardu was amazed, "A hundred rupees a day?"

Ranveer affirmed, "Yes, you don't even get that much for a day's labor. Over there, they'll just be taking care of a child."

Bhikaram and Hardu understood that at that time, the daily wage for labor was only sixty rupees, making a hundred rupees for babysitting a very attractive offer.

Ranveer pressed, "With money, you can advance in life; otherwise, nothing will come your way. If you follow that grocery shop boy's advice, you'll end up regressing. You won't know how far you'll go or where you'll end up—just think about it. The decision is yours."

Saying this, Ranveer stood up and started to leave. Hardu and Bhika followed him to the vehicle. As Ranveer got into the car, he said, "Alright, we'll leave; the rest is up to you..."

The next evening, Manoj was waiting for the two girls on the field, but neither showed up. Manoj was unaware of the changing circumstances. As he waited, he started to break blades of grass, then began jogging and stretching. A lot of time passed, and when the girls still hadn't arrived, he began to wander around. After waiting for a long time, as the sun began to set, Manoj left in despair.

He headed towards the Musahar settlement. Standing outside Lakhaniya and Baby's house, he called out, "Lakhaniya, Baby, is anyone there? Hardu Kaka, Bhika Kaka, is anyone around?"

Hardu and Bhika heard the call from inside. Just then, Baby rushed out, but Bhika pulled her back inside.

Bhika said, "Where are you going? Sit right here..."

As Hardu started to come outside, Bhika warned him, "Be careful; the snake must be killed without breaking the stick."

Hardu came outside and said, "Manoj bhaiya, the girls have found work; they won't be able to come running anymore."

Manoj said, "But we had agreed; it's just for two months. If they participate in the district-level games, the future will open up for them."

Hardu replied, "Brother, a poor man dreams of a coin in his sleep. We have to think about the wages we have in hand today..."

Manoj argued, "But..."

Hardu cut him off, "But nothing, brother. You're all big people; we don't even have the status to sit with you. If something goes wrong, it'll become a new problem. We humbly apologize."

Manoj grabbed Hardu's hands, saying, "No, Kaka, you don't understand. The arrival of these two girls can bring about a significant change."

Bhika came out just then.

Bhika said, "We don't want any change; we just want peace. Both girls have new jobs, and they'll earn a hundred rupees every day."

Manoj insisted, "But listen to my..."

Before Manoj could finish, Hardu and Bhika joined their hands and went back into the hut.

Manoj stood outside their hut for a while, pondering seriously.

Manoj thought, "If I give them a hundred rupees a day... will they send them then?"

Hearing this, the others standing there looked at Manoj in surprise. Manoj repeated his offer two or three times, prompting Hardu and Bhika to come back outside. Lakhaniya and Baby also listened from inside, realizing for the first time that Manoj Bhaiya was willing to go to any lengths.

After listening to Manoj, Hardu and Bhikha thought for a while and then said...

Bhikha - For sure, Hardu - We need the money every day; if we don't get it one day, then the girls won't come. Manoj quickly responded - For sure. So, the girls should come on time to run from tomorrow; when they return, I'll give both of you the money.

As Manoj was about to leave and moved ahead from the settlement, Lakhaniya and Baby stealthily came up to him from behind. Baby called out - Manoj Bhaiya, Manoj turned around to see both girls in front of him. Lakhaniya - You've acted completely crazy, Bhaiya. Our father will take money from you in our name and drink himself. Manoj – Dreams have to be paid for somehow... this is just the beginning. Baby - Where will you get the money from? Manoj - Don't worry about that; just tell me, do you both want to run with full effort or are you feeling weak inside?

Lakhaniya - Hey, do we have any other option, Manoj Bhaiya...

Baby - Now is the time to do something in life...

Manoj - I just wanted to hear this from both of you; if you both are with me, then we will surely do something better.

Now, Manoj faced a big challenge. On one hand, Gudiya was going to become a mother, and money was needed for her check-up, and on the other hand, he had to pay wages to Lakhaniya and Baby's father. If he abandoned the plan for running for a few days, it would be very difficult to involve both girls in this campaign later. Manoj's financial situation was extremely weak; he couldn't cover the expenses from the shop. There were only one and a half months left for the district-level running competition. In this situation, Manoj decided to borrow twenty thousand rupees from Chandan to quickly turn the circumstances in his favor.

That night, Gudiya was folding clothes and putting them in the cupboard when Manoj came and sat there quietly. Gudiya - What happened? You're sitting very quietly... How will you get the test done in the city... there's so much money needed. Manoj - I went to make arrangements there... Gudiya - How? Manoj - I've asked Chandan for twenty thousand...

Gudiya - That much? Manoj - Yes, I have some other work too... Gudiya - What other work is there...? Manoj – Whatever will be spent on your check-up, the remaining amount will have to be spent on training.

Gudiya - The doctor said the check-up would only cost up to four thousand. What will you do with the rest... spend it all on training? That's not much...

Manoj understands Gudiya's hesitation. Manoj - Actually, there's one problem. Lakhaniya and Baby will only come to run if I give their father a hundred rupees for labor every day...

Gudiya - Oh... what's this? First, teach them to play, and on top of that, give them money. What will you get? The world will laugh at you for being such a foolish man.

When Manoj didn't respond to Gudiya's remark, after a moment she asked herself. You have to give it separately to both the girls? Manoj – Yes, that's what I discussed with Hardu and Bhikha now.

Gudiya - Parents spend thousands on their children, and they are demanding the opposite... and you are also great to agree to give...

Manoj – If they understood this much, then why would this trouble arise...

Gudiya - Later, how will you give this money to Chandan? You'll also need money for the delivery of the baby, then where will you ask for it from...

Manoj – I haven't thought about that yet; I'm just thinking that these girls should somehow win the district-level sports competition next month.

Gudiya - Look, whatever you are doing, I am not against it, but if what you are thinking doesn't happen, remember you will land in new troubles. Now we are living a family life. A baby is coming; expenses are increasing, there's no income, and the shop isn't running. You're not able to give the shop full time. Think about whether playing sports is right or just a waste of time and money. I'm not stopping you, nor am I breaking your spirit. Still, I want you to think carefully before making a decision. There shouldn't be something that puts us into a new trouble. You are more educated than us; whatever you do, do it after careful consideration. Whatever will happen will be God's will.

# Chapter 16

Manoj didn't want to back down now. He was fully dedicated to preparing Lakhaniya and Baby for the district-level games. He knew that to go a long distance, one must take small steps; covering long distances in a single breath is almost impossible. Through training and exercise, he was not only boosting the girls' stamina but also continuously improving their technique and performance capability. After returning from training each day, Lakhaniya and Baby would give the money they received from Manoj to Hardu and Bhikhu.

One day, while all three were practicing, Manoj said with deep eyes - Sometimes years pass, but nothing changes in life; sometimes, in just a few days, so much changes that it remains an example for many years to come.

Upon hearing this, Lakhaniya and Baby's eyes lit up, and they were filled with enthusiasm. Manoj didn't want to let go of any self-control and discipline in their preparation.

After a whole month of hard work, Manoj brought Lakhaniya and Baby to the district sports office. The district sports office was organizing the upcoming district-level running competition. The competition was to take place just three days later.

Manoj took the form from there and filled it out for both girls. Manoj – Please submit this form. Clerk - Who are the players? Manoj - These two.

Clerk - There's no name of a school or club.

Manoj - Actually, both have studied up to the eighth grade, and they have been dropouts for the last two years; they have recently enrolled back in the ninth grade. They will run in the independent category now.

The clerk took the form in his hand, examined it closely, and then began completing the paperwork. While working, the clerk spoke.

Clerk - Have they ever run in any school or competition? Where did they receive training? Manoj – I am training them; they haven't run from school, but they won a race in the village a few days ago.

Clerk - Laughs - You won a race in the village, so you came here to register. Big school kids come here, practice for a year, and there's tough competition...

Manoj took both girls outside from the registration counter and reached the ground connected to the sports office where the competition was to take place. Manoj was with both girls, and they were seeing the sports field for the first time. Their eyes were wide open in astonishment at the circular track made for running. They couldn't believe that they had come to stand as full-fledged athletes in the competition today. ... Many girls were already practicing there. Their coaches were also present. Just then, Manoj said to both girls.

Manoj: You both will have race here tomorrow; you both should practice a bit here to get a feel for the ground.

Upon hearing this, both girls began stretching. Manoj went over to the coach who was training the other girls in running to gather some important information. After a while, Manoj signaled for the two girls to join him.

Manoj: You both will run two sets with those girls... It'll help you get a sense of the ground. This is very important.

The other girls there were in shorts, looking rough and tough, very smart. Some were from big convent schools, while others were from sports schools. Among the practicing girls, Lakhaniya and Baby were dressed in a rather peculiar manner. Both were wearing salwar and kurta, with the sports shoes Manoj had given them. Their hair was smeared with mustard oil, and they had tied their hair in braids with red ribbons. They also had long dupattas draped across their chests, which they had tied around their waists.

After some time, Baby and Lakhaniya stood with the other girls for the practice race. As soon as the count of three was completed, all the girls started running. Since Lakhaniya and Baby didn't understand the track well, Lakhaniya had trouble passing the girls ahead of her. During this, the dupatta tied around Lakhaniya's waist came undone, and her foot got caught in it. Lakhaniya stumbled and fell, and in a matter of seconds, the other girls had already run quite far ahead. Baby stopped to help Lakhaniya. Manoj noticed that the other girls had pulled far ahead. Lakhaniya's dupatta had torn, and because she had fallen, her pajama had also ripped from the bottom. She had scratches on her legs, and a little blood was oozing out.

Manoj ran over to them, and the other girls' coach also rushed there. Both girls were taken out of the track and made to sit down.

Other Coach: They still need a lot of practice. Teach them first, then bring them here.

Manoj: That's true.

The other coach left. Both girls felt like they had ruined all their hard work. Lakhaniya was more scared of the injury; she worried that Manoj might decide not to let her participate in the competition anymore. Baby comforted her. Just then, Manoj returned.

Manoj: You both sit here; I'll take a lap around the ground.

Manoj ran two laps around the ground. The two girls were sitting there. After a while, Manoj returned, running to them.

Manoj: Come on... we still have a lot to learn.

Hearing Manoj's words, both girls felt nervous; they thought their fears had come true.

The next day, the sports field was prepared, and the girls from other schools, who were going to race, had already arrived at the ground. School children had come as spectators to cheer for their school athletes. Then Manoj arrived with Lakhaniya and Baby, but that day was special. Lakhaniya and Baby were in shorts today. The girls with whom Lakhaniya and Baby had raced the previous day were looking at them in surprise.

Manoj, Baby, and Lakhaniya entered the ground with complete confidence. The race preparations were complete. Alongside the other girls, Lakhaniya and Baby were also standing on the track. The first event was the 100-meter race. As soon as the gunshot rang out, the race began, and in a flash, Lakhaniya and Baby sped past all the other girls. Lakhaniya came in first, and Baby second.

Overjoyed, they jumped up and hugged Manoj. He wholeheartedly encouraged both of them.

Moments later, Lakhaniya was back on the track tying her shoelaces, with Baby standing beside her. The 200-meter race was about to begin. As soon as this race started, the results were evident in a few moments, and the sports event committee's announcer was shouting into the mic that, surprisingly, Lakhaniya Kumari had also won the 200-meter race in first place. Baby Kumari was just a short distance behind in second place.

Minutes later, the results of the 400-meter race were announced, revealing that Baby Kumari had taken the lead, with Lakhaniya Kumari in second place.

A few minutes later, the results of the final 800-meter race were also out, and the announcer was astonished, announcing that Baby Kumari had once again secured victory, with Lakhaniya Kumari in second place. Both girls had run in a manner that was hard to believe; the announcer stated he had never seen any athlete win continuously like this in a single day in his lifetime. The other players present at the sports field and their coaches were perplexed as to which express train was running on the track. The spectators had not anticipated such an unexpected performance and wanted to know about these two unknown girls—who they were.

The coaches of other girls stood calmly, welcoming the victory.

After winning the match, both girls took photos with the trophy in hand. They held the trophies in both hands, and Manoj stood between them. Behind them, the organizers of the sports competition were standing, and a photo was clicked in this position. The next day, the photos appeared in all the major newspapers of the district with interesting headlines:

- New Sensation of Racing in the District

- Two New Flying Fairies in the Sports Competition

- Flying Girls Writing a New Chapter of Victory

After their photos appeared in the newspapers, Manoj and both girls became a sensation among the common people. Chandan and Sudarshan Chacha had come to Manoj's house and they were drinking tea, Chandan was reading the news loudly, published in the newspaper. Gudiya stood nearby, covering her head with her scarf.

Chandan: Manoj Pandey, an athlete trainer from Panchayat Phoolpur, along with Lakhaniya Kumari and Baby Kumari, has created a sensation in the district games by winning all the matches decisively. When asked about this success, Manoj Pandey stated that this is just the beginning; the destination is still far away. Lakhaniya Kumari and Baby Kumari are from very poor families in Manoj's village. Both girls are excited about their victory and will prepare themselves for the upcoming state-level competitions under their trainer Manoj Pandey.

Gudiya: Wow, Manoj bhaiya, you've created quite the atmosphere.

Sudarshan Chacha: The results are encouraging so far. What's the strategy moving forward?

Manoj: I have some plans in mind, Chacha ji...

Just then, there was a knock at the door. Gudiya opened it to find several villagers, including Hardu, Bhikha, and women from the Musahar settlement. Hardu and Bhikha stood with their hands folded, and Lakhaniya and Baby were with them.

As soon as Manoj came out...

Hardu: Manoj bhaiya, please forgive us; we have troubled you a lot.

Bhikharam: You are taking our daughter so far ahead, and instead of supporting you, we started asking you for money.

Hardu: Manoj bhaiya, we no longer need any money from you; these two girls are now in your hands. Prepare them as you wish; we will fully support you.

Manoj takes Hardu's hand and says, "Oh uncle, what are you doing?"Then some men arrived, including those from other villages. They began speaking to Manoj, saying that he should train not only Lakhaniya and Baby but also the other girls in the village. They had come from the Manakapur Panchayat after reading about him in the newspaper and wanted him to train their girl as well. "Whatever support you need from us, we will provide."

Manoj: You all have trusted us; that's our strength. Now we will move forward together and create a new future for our children. When their dreams come true, our dreams will automatically come true.

# Chapter 17

When someone achieves success, their success lights the path for the dreams of others. The small success of Manoj, Lakhaniya, and Baby had filled many nearby girls and their families with courage. Many families now wanted to send their daughters to Manoj for training. Manoj was also expanding the training within his limited capacity. In the next six months, Lakhaniya and Baby made a mark in inter-district and zonal competitions as well. Some other girls were also preparing for district-level games. Newspapers began to publish the story of Manoj and the girls receiving training from him every day. Lakhaniya and Baby had emerged as star players and had gained significant recognition in the surrounding areas. Their photos were often published holding trophies after winning races.

One day, Ranveer's Tata Sumo was driving down the village's unpaved road. Three boys riding a bullet came from the opposite direction, acting like heroes. As the boys passed in front of Ranveer's car, he called out to them.

Ranveer: Hey Sandeep, listen!

The bullet carrying the boys stopped a little ahead of Ranveer's vehicle, but then they reversed their vehicle.

The boy driving the bullet, Sandeep, dragged the bullet backward while seated. Two boys sat behind, and the weight of their presence was preventing the bullet from moving. Sandeep, feeling frustrated, spoke to the boys sitting behind.

Sandeep: Get down, you fools! How will the bullet go back with you two sitting there?

Both boys quickly got down. Now both vehicles were facing each other.

Meanwhile, Ranveer spoke to Sandeep, sitting in the Tata Sumo.

Ranveer: How are you, Sandeep?

Sandeep: Greetings, brother!

Ranveer: Sandeep, I have recommended you for the position of District Youth Leader. Your name will probably be announced soon.

Upon hearing this, Sandeep felt happy.

Sandeep: Thank you so much, brother! It's because of you that this wish of mine is coming true.

Ranveer: You see, there are many thorns on the path to progress. Sometimes you have to remove them, and sometimes you have to endure them.

Sandeep: Yes, brother!

Ranveer: Let's do this: organize a youth meeting the day after tomorrow.

Sandeep: Where? At the district office?

Ranveer: No, that won't work. Strength comes from rising from your own home. Do it in your village. People will come from the district level.

While Sandeep and Ranveer were talking, vehicles coming from both directions on that road had stopped. Sandeep and Ranveer's people were signaling to those coming from both sides to stop.

Sandeep: Yes, brother, but there isn't much space in the village.

Ranveer: Oh come on! Are you asking where the water is when you're at the well? That boy from the Pandit's family races everyone in your field, earning thousands, and you're asking where the space is?

Sandeep: Yes, that is true.

Ranveer: Hold the event there. Set up a tent by the day after tomorrow, and make sure the boy from the Pandit's family doesn't play on your land.

As soon as Ranveer spoke this, his driver and other followers began to laugh. Sandeep felt embarrassed.

Ranveer's car moved ahead.

After talking to Ranveer, Sandeep went straight to his field where Manoj trained his athletes

On the field, Lakhaniya and Baby were already practicing. A couple of other girls were there, but Manoj hadn't arrived yet. Lakhaniya was teaching a new girl stretching exercises. All the girls were wearing shorts and were exercising without any worries.

Baby: Hey Lakhaniya, Manoj bhaiya hasn't come yet.

Lakhaniya: He said he would be a little late. He is going to the hospital with bhabhi...

Just then, Sandeep came thundering onto the field on his bullet and started riding it around the girls.

Seeing the sudden arrival of the boys, the girls began to look at Sandeep closely. Lakhaniya didn't like the boys' behavior, so she quickly spoke up.

Lakhaniya: What's going on...?

Sandeep: What's wrong with you? Isn't it hot...?

One of the boys sitting behind Sandeep said, "Brother, wearing half pants only makes it hotter."

After saying this, all three boys began to stare at the girls' thighs. The girls practicing became disturbed by the boys' behavior. To support Lakhaniya, Baby stepped forward and said.

Baby: What's the problem...?

Sandeep stopped the bullet and got down.

Sandeep: By tending goats, your status has risen, and you think you can become a heroine...?

The girls were still quietly listening.

Sandeep: This land is ours, on which you're jumping...

Lakhaniya: It is fine, but who is taking the land away?

Sandeep: No more jumping around here from tomorrow... That Pandit, what's his name? Manoj? You should tell him not to jump anywhere else... or else...

Baby: Or else...

A boy who came with Sandeep added, "Or else you'll have to jump on the bed with brother." Saying this, the boy placed his hand on Baby's breast.

As soon as the boy touched Baby, she slapped him hard.

As soon as he was slapped, the boy lunged at Baby... Seeing Baby getting beaten, Lakhaniya also confronted that boy. As Lakhaniya confronted him, Sandeep and another boy joined in the fight. Baby and Lakhaniya, along with the girls practicing, were confused about what to do in this situation. Some girls began to scream and make noise. When they saw that no help was coming, they got scared and started to run away. Meanwhile, Lakhaniya and Baby were fiercely confronting the rowdy boys.

The boys were three in number, so they had the upper hand, but the two girls weren't backing down either. Suddenly, one of the boys took out a knife and lunged at Lakhaniya, while the other boys began to pull Baby by her hair.

Sandeep: Drag that whore into the bushes; I'll make her jump high today.

Chela: Come on, you bitch...

Baby and Lakhaniya screamed. One boy started trying to pull off Baby's shorts when suddenly a powerful punch landed on his face. That boy fell back. Manoj had arrived. The girls who had run away had informed Manoj about the entire incident, and he had come running.

Now Manoj and the two girls confronted Sandeep and his boys with full force, and they severely beat them up. People working in the other fields ran to the scene and managed to stop the fight between the two sides.

Just a few minutes later, both sides were accusing each other in front of the police officer at the station. Sandeep accused Manoj of trying to illegally occupy his land under the pretext of training the girls, and when he tried to stop Manoj, he attacked him with the girls. Meanwhile, Manoj and the girls claimed that Sandeep had attempted to force himself on the girls. The police officer seemed to side with Sandeep as several local leaders had called in his support.

The officer said to Manoj, "If you forcibly intrude into his land, anyone will try to stop you."

Manoj: That is not true; we only go there for practice; the girls are preparing for state-level running.

Sandeep: So why do you come to my land?

Manoj: There's no field in the village, so  needed a proper place to run for practice...

Station Head: Oh, if you want to practice than you can hold anyone's land?

Manoj: You're misunderstanding.

Station Head (shouting): And you're understanding correctly? I've been watching your arrogance for a long time; if I hit you with a stick, all your bravado will vanish.

Manoj was also getting angry, but Chandan held Manoj's shoulder and asked him to stay calm so things wouldn't escalate further. Baby and Lakhaniya were also silently standing there.

Sandeep: I'm saying, file an FIR against them.

Manoj: If you're filing an FIR against us, then file one against them too.

The Station Head, irritated, said to Manoj, "Do you think you are a big minister that I'll do everything you say? Munshi, take them inside and file an FIR against them. Get these girls inside too."

Seeing the situation slipping out of hand, Manoj took Chandan aside and gave him a number. After that, Chandan left the place. By then, two constables had taken Manoj by the arm and led him to the lockup, while the girls were made to sit outside.

Baby and Lakhaniya had also lost their composure—"Sandeep has been harassing us; he was trying molest us; don't let him go!"

Sandeep: Shut up, you!

Station Head to Sandeep: Hey, you be quiet; we're watching everything. Get everyone inside...

Now the Station Head and Sandeep started talking.

Manoj stood inside the lockup and both girls were looking at him from outside. A call came on the Station Head's basic phone after half an hour.

Station Head: Hello.

It was a call from the Superintendent of Police(SP)...

Station Head: Sir...

When the SP asked something, the Station Head quickly replied.

Station Head: Sir, the FIR hasn't been filed yet...

There was a muffled voice on the other end...

Station Head: No sir, you don't need to come; I'll handle everything...
Sir...

Then a voice came from the other end, giving a final order, and the call ended. After that, the Station Head put down the phone, addressing the Munshi to bring those people in. Sandeep was sitting there, confused by this sudden change. Manoj came out of the lockup in front of the Station Head.

Station Head: Manoj babu, you shouldn't go playing in their land anymore... Make some alternative arrangements; if you can't, let us know...

Manoj: I've already said that we'll arrange something else; these people are just escalating a pointless conflict.

Station Head: No problem, now you can go home; take both girls with you, and we guarantee that they won't disturb you anymore. Is that okay?

Manoj: Yes, thank you very much...

Manoj came out of the police station with both girls. Outside the station, a crowd had gathered, and several people, including Hardu and Bhiku, were standing there. Sudarshan Chacha and Chandan were also there with everyone. Manoj headed back to the village. After Manoj and the girls left the police station, Sandeep immediately asked the Station Head.

Sandeep: Your attitude changed as soon as the phone call came.

Station Head, lighting a cigarette: It was the SP's call; He knew we hadn't filed the FIR yet and said that if we were to file it, we should do it for both parties.

Sandeep: Then file it for both parties; he's encroaching on our land!

Station Head: Oh man, you're such a fool; how will you become a leader? If we file FIRs for both parties, you would be charged with attempted rape for Dalit girls. You wouldn't get bail, and your political career would be over. The case would blow up so much that even your father wouldn't be able to handle it in this lifetime.

Sandeep is taken aback...

Station Head: You're trying to be a leader, but I have to educate you; sometimes compromising is better than taking revenge...

Meanwhile, Manoj was heading towards the village with both girls when they asked him.

Baby: How did this all happen, Manoj Bhaiya? We thought the inspector would send us to jail.

Chandan: How would he send us to jail? Manoj Bhaiya must have called the SP.

Manoj: Yes, I had a friend who studied with me in Delhi.

These days he's the SP in Madhya Pradesh, and his batch mate is the SP of our district. Everyone was walking towards the village in the dim light, discussing how help is never in vain; even if you don't get anything immediately in return, God will come back to help you in some form when needed. Everyone was now fully convinced of this.

The next day, there was a meeting at Manoj's house to discuss the police station incident. Chandan, Sudarshan Chacha, Lakhaniya, and Baby were all present. Gudiya brought tea for everyone, covering her belly with her sari pallu due to her pregnancy. Chandan and Manoj were talking. Everyone agreed that if you do something good, there will always be some opposition. Manoj said they needed to find an alternative to the ground. Just then, Gudiya asked, "Why are these two girls worried?"

Lakhaniya: Bhabi, those are all rascals; we know that. They're not going to stop here.

Manoj interrupted Lakhaniya, saying, "But if we don't move forward now, we'll be pushed back... History shows that those who didn't try to rise were oppressed even more."

Chandan: But the question now is, what should we do?

Manoj said that for now, we just needed to focus on the state championship. We had to reach Kolkata by the morning after tomorrow. They would think about what to do after coming back. The other girls coming for training should be told that Manoj Bhaiya has gone to Kolkata. When he returns, he will meet everyone, and until then, everyone should continue with light exercises at home.

Chandan: When is the train?

Manoj: Tomorrow morning. After this, Manoj told both girls to get ready because they were leaving tomorrow morning. Hearing this, both girls left.

Chandan got up with Manoj and asked him, "Hey, the time for your wife's delivery is coming, and you're leaving?"

Manoj immediately understood the seriousness of Chandan's question. He replied, "Yes, I have that dilemma too. If I don't go, all the hard work of both girls will go to waste, and the path ahead will be completely closed. After coming this far, it would be very wrong to miss this opportunity."

Chandan: I'm here, but it's better for a husband to be with his wife during delivery. Every wife wants that.

Manoj: I'll think about it, but for now, let's assume I'm leaving tomorrow, so you should go now; we need to head to the station in the morning. We shouldn't miss the train.

Chandan: I'll take the car to Bishunpur Market early in the morning. After that, I'll take you to the station.

Manoj: Then how will you come back?

Chandan: I'll go early in the morning, and I'll return before you all leave; then I'll drop you all at the station in that car.

Manoj: Alright.

Chandan had left. Meanwhile, Gudiya was listening to their conversation from behind the door. When Manoj lay down on the bed, Gudiya came to the doorway and said, "Since you've already decided to go, why did you need to tell Chandan Bhaiya that you'll think about it?"

Manoj: If you say, I can stop, but it's very important for me to go.

Gudiya: What kind of answer is that? Can going anywhere be more important than your child?

At Gudiya's remark, Manoj thought for a moment before responding, "It's not more important than the child, but the current situation is under my control, and even if everything is fine, if I don't go with the girls, all my hard work will go to waste."

Gudiya was annoyed by this answer: "And what if things go wrong here?"

Manoj: The doctor has given an appointment for ten days later... I'll be back in three days anyway. Besides, you haven't had any problems.

Gudiya: Will the child arrive exactly at the time the doctor has mentioned? And just because there haven't been problems before doesn't mean there won't be any now.

Manoj got frustrated: "What do you want? Just tell me if I should go or if I should cancel everything."

Gudiya: Why should I stop you? Don't you have any sense?

Manoj: I cannot put the responsibility of those two girls on anyone else. Whatever happens, we'll see. After the clash with Sandeep, I definitely can't do that. If they go to Calcutta, I won't know where they are or what they are doing, and if something goes wrong, I won't be able to forgive myself, and people will lose trust in me.

Gudiya: Fine, if you want to do what you feel like, go ahead. If you want to go to Calcutta to earn people's trust, remember that if something goes wrong here, you'll break your wife's trust, and you don't seem to care about that at all.

Both lay on their respective sides of the bed without speaking for a long time. Sleep was absent from their eyes, and they were both trying to give the impression to each other that they had fallen asleep.

The next morning, as dawn broke, both girls got ready and came to Manoj's house, where Manoj was standing before them.

Manoj told the girls, "Look, the schedule has changed a bit. Your Bhabhi is in labor, and I might need to be here. In this case, Chandan will go with you both." Upon hearing this, both girls became somewhat uncomfortable.

Manoj understood their discomfort: "What happened?"

Baby: But Manoj bhaiya, if you don't come and we face any shortcomings in practice or play, will chandan bhaiya be able to resolve the issue, right?

Lakhaniya quickly grasped the situation and spoke to manage it: "Oh, no, Bhaiya, you've made so many preparations, we won't make any mistakes. Your presence here is also important."

Manoj felt confused; he didn't want to put the girls' safety and game responsibilities on anyone else. He was in a moral dilemma.

Baby: But where is Chandan Bhaiya?

Manoj: He must be coming with the vehicle; we talked last night. Everyone is waiting for Chandan... Manoj and Gudiya weren't speaking to each other. The girls started a conversation to lighten the mood, trying to show that they were completely at ease about going to Calcutta and were ready for the game. But inside, they were also getting anxious. Meanwhile, the train's departure time was approaching, yet Chandan hadn't shown up yet... Manoj kept glancing at the clock. Gudiya was also coming and going in between. Manoj waited for Chandan until the last moment, and when he didn't arrive, he stood up.

Manoj: If we wait any longer for Chandan, we'll miss the train; who knows where he has gone. Saying this, Manoj quickly packed two pairs of clothes into a bag. Seeing this, both girls also slung their bags over their shoulders.

Manoj: Go inside and tell Bhabi that we're leaving. Let her know that I'm with you, and if Chandan arrives in the meantime, send him directly to the station.

Lakhaniya went inside. Gudiya had already heard everything because she had been paying attention to their conversation.

Lakhaniya: Bhabi, Bhaiya...

Gudiya: I've heard everything; you all go. Play well.

The next moment, the three of them left the house, and Gudiya watched them as they went.

As Manoj set out with the two girls in a village tempo towards the railway station, Chandan rushed into Manoj's house.

Chandan, in a hurry, called out, "Manoj, have you left? Bhabi, Bhabi, Bhabi..." Calling out, looked inside the house and saw Gudiya lying unconscious on the ground.

Chandan picked Gudiya up and rushed her to the hospital. He realized that Manoj had already left for the station. At the hospital, the doctor asked Chandan, "Who are you to her?"

Chandan: She's my friend's wife.

Doctor: Where is her husband?

Chandan: He left for Calcutta today.

Doctor: Oh, there's a lot of bleeding; she might need blood.

Chandan got startled: "Doctor, is everything else alright?"

Doctor: Just arrange for blood; otherwise, everything won't be fine. Go meet the nurse at the counter; she'll tell you what to do.

Chandan ran towards the nurse. Meanwhile, Manoj was sitting in the train's sleeper compartment with both girls, who were looking out at the fields and laughing together. Manoj was sitting there in deep concern, weighing his decision to leave Gudiya alone. He felt he had made the wrong choice, but he had to make a decision. Often, situations arise where no matter what decision you make, one party is always upset, and you become the unwitting culprit.

# Chapter 18

Upon reaching Calcutta, Manoj took both girls to the ground where the state-level championship was to take place. Both girls touched the ground with respect. The ground was bustling with girls who were already practicing, and the other players were watching them. Manoj told the girls, "Now that we've seen the ground, let's go wash up and rest a bit." After this, Manoj and the girls went to their allotted rooms in the state playground's hostel to drop off their bags.

A few hours later, the three returned to the ground and began light jogging. The championship was scheduled for the next day, so Manoj had taken the girls to the ground to gather technical information. While jogging, Manoj was providing the girls with technical insights about the upcoming game. After running a few laps, they all stopped at one spot.

Manoj knew well that to win, a whole system needs to work effectively. But they had limited resources. In this scenario, Lakhaniya and Baby needed more internal motivation, discipline, hard work, and dedication to their goals than any external system. He believed that they had worked well on all these parameters, and when someone performs well according to these standards, the chances of favorable results increase. Now, at this final moment, all that was left was to run with full strength, for which he was preparing both girls.

Manoj: Just like a lion puts in its full effort when hunting, you need to run with all your might. Do you both understand?

Lakhaniya: Yes, we understand.

Baby: Let's see what luck has in store.

Manoj scolded her: "No, after all this hard work, such thoughts shouldn't come up. These thoughts weaken your morale."

Baby: Oh, I was just...

Manoj: Those who rely only on luck end up with the scraps that hard workers leave behind. You both have worked quite hard. Just avoid mistakes tomorrow and give it your all.

Meanwhile, in the village, Chandan went to the doctor: "Doctor, what is the situation now?"

Doctor: Look, brother, the baby is very weak; it's a premature baby, and its breathing is very rapid. It will need to stay in the incubator for four days, and after that, we will see if it needs to stay longer. We won't be able to say anything until then. For now, just pray that the baby stays safe.

Unaware of the turmoil happening in the village, the day of the championship had arrived in Kolkata, and Lakhaniya stood on the track with other female athletes. The stadium was packed with a huge crowd, and in just a few moments, the 200-meter race was about to begin. There was a difference in technique and timing between the two, and Manoj was aware of this quality. Therefore, he had registered Baby for long-distance races like the 800 meters and 1600 meters, while due to Lakhaniya's better timing, he had registered her for the 100 meters, 200 meters, and 400 meters.

Then, at that moment, as the gunshot rang out, all the athletes began to run, and amid intense competition, Lakhaniya won the 200-meter race. In the next competition, Baby also won the 800-meter race. Thus, both girls managed to meet expectations and secured victories in their respective competitions. Manoj looked extremely excited because the goal had been achieved. It was a miracle that both girls won in all events at the state-level championship. Manoj felt that his dream was now coming true, and the wounds of not being successful in his life were starting to heal. Today, he believed that many times, when a person wants to go in one direction but cannot, it simply means that another path is waiting for them.

Everyone must go through a phase filled with despair at some point in their lives, caught between immense effort and failure. During this time, a person feels that all their efforts are in vain and that nothing will happen. But then, the waves of life reveal themselves, showing the path where the destination starts to become visible.

Once again, Lakhaniya, Baby, and Manoj became the headlines in the newspapers, and the next day, many sports pages featured their photos and news. When news spreads, it travels far; the news of their victories had already reached their village even before them. Upon returning from Kolkata, Chandan and the villagers had come to greet both girls and Manoj at the railway station with great fanfare. Hardu and Bhikhu were also there. Manoj and both girls were celebrated with festivities from the railway station to the village. Manoj had already informed the village about the explosive victories of both girls over the phone.

The rest of the work was taken care of by the news in the newspapers the next day. Society worships success and tends to forget the negative aspects associated with successful individuals. After this success, new standards were set for Manoj, Lakhaniya, and Baby in their village and the surrounding area. People considered them inspirational and wanted to connect with them.

There is an old saying that everyone wants to make the winner their brother-in-law, while no one wants to associate with the loser. Well, a lot was about to change due to this victory, but Manoj still faced another problem. Manoj and Chandan were standing near a tree outside the hospital talking.

Manoj: "You are a fool man, do you have straw stuffed in your head? Why didn't you tell me such a big thing that the baby is in the incubator? I would have danced and sung like a madman coming home, thinking everything was fine."

Chandan: "Oh man, Bhabi had forbidden it, saying you would get disturbed."

Manoj: "Bhabi said... you'll destroy her devotion someday."

Chandan: "Why are you getting angry? Is it my fault? One cannot ride two boats at the same time. It was up to you to decide whether to see your wife and child first or to go play in Kolkata. I reminded you that night to think about what you wanted to do. I handled the situation in your absence, and you are getting upset with me."

Listening to Chandan, Manoj fell silent and, gathering himself, spoke to him.

Manoj: "Anyway, what does the doctor say now?"

Chandan: "The baby's condition has improved; the doctor said they would discharge her tomorrow."

Manoj: "Chandan brother, you had already helped me with twenty thousand rupees before, and now this expense has come upon you again. I don't even have the money to return your old amount, and now this new expense has come up. Brother, I'm in no position to say anything. I haven't been able to clear my father's debt completely yet."

Chandan took Manoj's hand. "Don't think about all this, Manoj. You keep trying; you are making good efforts, and you are yielding results. I'm sure you will soon turn the situation in your favor. Money comes and goes. Once your work is done, the money will come again."

Manoj felt grateful for Chandan's faith; he understood well that in times when brothers are killing each other over money, if someone starts spending from their limited income to help you fulfill your dreams, no one could be a better well-wisher than that.

After meeting Chandan, Manoj went inside the hospital and saw that Gudiya was sound asleep on the hospital bed. Manoj quietly approached and, after looking at Gudiya for a while, gently squeezed her limp hand.

Gudiya startled: "What happened?" she said softly, recognizing Manoj as he approached.

Manoj: "Forgive me."

Gudiya: "For what...?"

Manoj: "For leaving my responsibilities and running away."

Gudiya did not want to prolong the conversation and said, "Everything will be alright."

Gudiya gently squeezed Manoj's hands. Manoj sat down next to Gudiya, feeling heavy with regret. He felt that if something had happened to the baby, how could he have forgiven himself? Gudiya told Manoj to go see their daughter. The nurse would show her to him from outside. After this, Manoj went with Chandan to see their daughter. Seeing his daughter in the incubator, Manoj became extremely emotional. He then went straight to the doctor.

The doctor said they would discharge the baby as soon as her breathing was normal, but she would need to be taken care of for at least one month. Manoj suddenly felt a deep sense of responsibility—the responsibility of being a father.

The feeling of fatherhood arises late in a man because he cannot feel the child developing in the womb. In contrast, a woman's sense of motherhood begins the moment the baby comes into the womb. Although a man may experience this feeling later, when it arises, it is profound. A man can encompass his identity, preferences, freedom, and priorities within the feeling of fatherhood, binding it happily to the limits of his family, and he pulls it along like a bull, nurturing it like a farmer.

# Chapter 19

A few months had passed, and Manoj and Gudiya's child had grown a few months older. The child's health had improved. Manoj had stopped training the girls for a month after the birth of the child, but he had started looking for a new place to train the girls, and in the meantime, he was giving basic training to the girls on a small piece of vacant land near Chandan's house. However, he knew that this arrangement wouldn't solve the problem, and such preparation would not adequately prepare the athletes. The problem was exacerbated because after the fight with Sandeep, there was a negative campaign in the village suggesting that if land was given for training the girls, Manoj might seize it later. Some people agreed to let Manoj use the land for training only on the condition that he would pay rent monthly. In such dire circumstances, it was not possible for Manoj to manage that, and he did not want to charge any fees from the girls coming for training.

Manoj was worried that if the training remained suspended for a long time, it would be very challenging to prepare the children physically and mentally for it, and many girls might distance themselves from the training. Some girls might find other jobs, or their families might discourage them from training, pushing them to engage in other activities.

The girls who trained under Manoj mostly belonged to a poor class, where living was based on the principle of "dig a well every day and drink water." Their daily income depended on daily wages. If they didn't earn daily, getting food could become difficult. After holding back training for several days due to these dilemmas, Manoj decided to give basic training to the children on a quiet road in the village until a permanent arrangement for training could be made. He set a time of five in the morning for all the children so that training could be conducted easily on the deserted road. However, the issue was that many girls did household chores in the morning, such as Baby and

Lakhaniya, who went to the market to sell vegetables. Similarly, many girls did other jobs that were necessary for their family's livelihood. Training in the evening was not possible due to the arrival and departure of vehicles on the road. As a result, many girls were unable to attend the training. Another problem was the risk of injury during training on the road, which made it difficult to perform many exercises that were essential for stamina and strength. All these concerns were troubling Manoj, but he couldn't find a solution due to the lack of alternatives.

One day, Gudiya was massaging her child when Manoj was sitting outside in the sun, fixing some things on the cot, and then Chandan called out from outside.
Manoj: Yes, come in...

Chandan entered the house with quick steps and told Manoj that some people had come to meet him and were waiting outside. Some people from a sports agency had come with Chandan that day,. The manager of that agency was named Pritam Singh, who had come to the village to meet Manoj, accompanied by his colleagues.
Manoj welcomed all of them inside and asked them to sit on the cot in the courtyard. Seeing the unfamiliar faces, Gudiya took the child and went inside.

Pritam Singh: Hello, Manoj Ji, you don't know us, but we know you. What you have accomplished is being talked about in every sports academy.
Manoj: I don't understand.

Pritam: Actually, we have a company called India Rising Sports. Our company manufactures sports-related products and sponsors athletes who are consistently performing well, ensuring that they don't face any issues in their sport. We read about you, Lakhaniya, and Baby in the newspaper when you won the state championship in Calcutta. Manoj was surprised, as he didn't expect that someone would come to meet him after reading a news article.

Manoj asked Pritam Singh: So, tell me, what can I do for you? Pritam: You don't have to do anything; we will take care of everything. Just focus on your game and keep progressing. This raised another question for Manoj. He asked, "I don't understand what you mean. You will do everything, and we will just play our game? How is that possible, and why will you help us?"

Pritam: That's a very good question.

Chandan: So what's the right answer to this question? Pritam: The right answer is that the players who get selected will promote our products. They will do the marketing. Manoj: So, you mean you will do business with our game and profit from it?

Pritam: You will benefit as well, Sir. We will provide essential items for your training.

Manoj started to think.

Pritam: There's really nothing to think about here; it benefits both the players and the company. Even big players do the same. You are a good trainer; we have learned that your training has been halted for several months while you want to prepare good players. If good players are prepared, the game will develop. If the game develops, there will be a favourable environment for sports, branding will happen, a market will be created, and our company will thrive. In this scenario, Manoj Ji, our paths align. We are just walking down the same road with different goals.

After thinking for a while, Manoj said, "Please give me some time to think; then I will let you know." Pritam agreed to this. Pritam: Take your time, and here's my card. Call me at the number on it to talk to me. Along with this, here are the details of our plan; please read it. There's no rush to respond, but don't delay so much that waiting becomes unbearable.

Chandan took the card and brochure.

That night, Chandan and Manoj were discussing together.

Chandan: What have you thought? Did you read that book they gave about their company?

Manoj: What book did they give?

Chandan: That shiny one with two or four pages filled with a lot of photos and information.

Manoj: Oh, that brochure.

Chandan: Yes, that one.

Manoj: But that's not called a book.

Chandan got annoyed, saying, "Now let's argue about what to call it; I just want to know if you've read it." Manoj started laughing and then replied, "Yes, I've looked through all the papers. The company works in sports."

Chandan, irritated: Then what?

Manoj: Look, if these people can solve the ground issue and provide basic sports equipment for our kids' training, I have no objections. What else is in their minds will only become clear after talking to them. God guides those who want to try. It's the law of time that it will support those who dedicate time to determined efforts toward their goals, and those who don't will not be given opportunities by time.

Inspired by this, a few days later, fully prepared, Manoj, along with Chandan, went to meet Pritam Singh in Delhi. Manoj had come to the decision that there was no other option to start training girls in the village with full force. He had resolved in his mind that if the company had any unreasonable conditions that would negatively impact their goals, he would not enter into any agreement with them. Only after deciding all these matters, Manoj decide to meet Pritam Singh. They both went to Pritam Singh's office.

Pritam: Please come in.

Manoj: Yes, hello.

Pritam: I'm glad you came to meet me; I was feeling that I would meet you in a few days. Please sit, would you like tea or coffee?

Chandan: Let's have both.

Manoj interrupts Chandan: No, we won't take anything.

Pritam: So, what do you think about our offer?

Manoj: Look, we have two basic needs right now. First, there isn't a single ground in the village; if some arrangement could be made for a ground in the village so that the players can practice there.

Pritam: And what's the second?

Manoj: The second need is that the necessary sports equipment should be available for the players to prepare properly.

Pritam: Look, Manoj Ji, I respect your efforts very much, but I want to inform you that the two demands you're making are essential for any athlete's preparation.

Manoj: Yes.

Pritam: While you might refer to them as two demands, in a way, this constitutes the entire setup.

Chandan: We will provide training, right...?

Pritam: You will provide training, but how will you do it without infrastructure? That's the question.

Manoj: I agree with you. That's why we came to you; you said you wouldn't do anything, and we would do everything; we just need to play our game and move forward.

Pritam Singh started laughing.

Pritam: Well, let's get back to your requests. We agree with your demands, but how it will happen will take time to decide on the proposal letter.

Manoj: Alright, please prepare the proposal letter. There's one more question I want to understand. I still don't get what you expect from us in return. There must be some conditions or expectations from your side.

Pritam Singh said, "Don't worry; our conditions will be written in that proposal letter."

Manoj: Okay.

Pritam: You will have to sign it and give it to us; the rest we will handle.

Manoj and Chandan both got up and left Pritam's office. The next day, Manoj and Chandan received the offer letter. Both were discussing whether to sign the offer letter. Chandan believed that Manoj should understand everything. After reading all the documents, Manoj felt assured from his side and thought a decision had to be made as there was no other option. After all, one should assess their capabilities to find a solution to the problem and choose an appropriate option from all available choices. The decision you make regarding your chosen option will determine whether your boat sinks in the storm or reaches the shore.

Manoj - Look, their first condition is that any girl from our academy who performs well in the National Games will promote their products.

Chandan - Does that mean no other company can sponsor their products?

Manoj - The situation is such that Pritam's company provides services to many companies. In this case, through our athletes, they will market those companies' products and charge a hefty fee from them. That's why they are inclined to invest in us.

Chandan - What does that mean? Will this be a permanent arrangement?

Manoj - No, this contract will only apply to the player who wins the National Games for the first two years. Look, Chandan, Pritam's company believes that a national player will emerge from here by next year, so they are betting on us now because it will be expensive to buy the winning player later. That's why they are placing their bets while it's still cheap.

Chandan - That's true; people do bet on winning horses. But what about the ground? They won't give us that.

Manoj - They have offered that if the land is mine, they will develop the infrastructure on it; otherwise, we can find another piece of land, and they will pay the rent for it.

Chandan - And if no player from our side makes it to the nationals, what will happen then? That's a possibility too.

Manoj - This contract is currently for one year; during this time, they can break it whenever they want. We don't have the right to break the contract. This is the only condition that, if there's a disagreement with this company, we won't be able to back out. But we have to think positively and play well; we shouldn't think there will be disagreements. They are also ready to pay rent for the land we take on lease, and they are willing to develop the basic structure for the game on that rented land.

Chandan - But the fact that we don't have the right to break the complicated things of the contract.

Manoj - Complicated? Chandan Babu, it's business. They say that if the investment is theirs, then they have the right to break the contract, not us.

Chandan - So, what will you do now?

Manoj - What can we do? There's no straightforward path to success. We have to take risks.

Chandan - What do you mean?

Manoj - Let's go ahead with this for now; we'll see the future as it comes.

After this, Manoj signed the proposal and sent the original copy to Pritam in a large envelope.

# Chapter – 20

After the agreement was finalized, Manoj found a piece of land in the village and had already negotiated the rent with the owners. He informed Pritam Singh about it. A team from Pritam Singh's company was coming to the village to prepare designs for developing the infrastructure for training in the rented land, after consulting with Manoj. However, this team would only come if Manoj convinced Lakhaniya and Baby to sign the proposal, which stated that any player winning from Manoj's training institute in the future would have to endorse Pritam's company's products.

Manoj had been busy with all these arrangements for the past week when the postman arrived and handed him a registered letter. It was from the Sports Department, informing Manoj that Lakhaniya and Baby had been selected for the state-level team and had been invited to the state-level sports hostel for training. Upon reading this, a smile spread across Manoj's face. In life, being better is not always enough for victory; sometimes, winning requires taking a different approach and creating your own path.

The next day, Manoj was telling Lakhaniya and Baby about their selection and also informing them that he was negotiating with an agency to train other children so that players could be prepared while staying in the village. For this, both of them would need to sign a paper stating that if they were selected for the national team, they would promote the company's brand. If they did not do so, the company would not provide ground and sports equipment, and Manoj might have to abandon the plan for training the other children.

Manoj explained that if any other player also reached the national level, they would also be bound by this agreement. This agreement was set to become a milestone for the development of sports in the village and for discovering new players. Lakhaniya and Baby considered Manoj their mentor and could not even think of disagreeing with him. They believed that he was the reason for their success, so they were willingly ready to sign the paper.

After Lakhaniya and Baby signed the agreement, the contract between Pritam's company and Manoj's company was finalized, and within a month, the land for sports training was fully prepared. In a way, Manoj's dream was very close to coming true, and the biggest issue of financial challenge seemed to be resolved.

Manoj was very happy. Meanwhile, Lakhaniya and Baby were joyfully bidding farewell for the sports college. As they were heading towards the sports college, Hardu came up to them and said, "Manoj Bhaiya has brought you this far. This feels like a dream coming true. Go ahead and make us proud with your hard work." Manoj had brought Lakhaniya and Baby to the sports hostel.

Their dream had come true; now they were recognized state-level players. After reaching the hostel, the two girls couldn't believe they had come this far. They were still struggling to accept how they had made it here. They recalled the days they used to rush to sell vegetables in the morning. Every student in the hostel was treating them like stars because everyone knew about their magical races.

When Manoj left the two girls at the hostel, he reminded them to work hard and avoid any distractions. Real success was still a long way off. Manoj was confident that both girls understood this well.

In the hostel, for the first time, the two girls felt a sense of freedom. They felt like free birds. They were laughing, singing, making their own decisions, and choosing things based on their preferences. They realized for the first time how beautiful freedom is. There were no worries; they just had to practice, which they were doing even when they had to arrange for food and earnings. So, being in the hostel and only training seemed like a piece of cake. During the rest of the time, they indulged in their hobbies. For the first time, both girls felt a shift from being laborers to embracing their femininity; they wanted to wear nice clothes and pay attention to their appearance. They couldn't believe they could also look beautiful. Before this, they had never seen themselves in that light.

All these things were on one side, but one thing was clear in both girls' minds: if they didn't play, everything would be taken away from them. Therefore, they didn't want to compromise at all regarding their performance in the game. They were practicing with complete focus and determination.

Meanwhile, Manoj had started a sports academy with the help of a company. He had brought Chandan along to help him. The success of Lakhaniya and Baby had inspired people from nearby villages, and they were sending their daughters in large numbers to Manoj's academy. Seeing such an organized academy was a pleasant experience for both the children and their families.

Girls from not just the village but also nearby urban areas were coming to Manoj's academy. Manoj had also repaid his debts that he had borrowed from Chandan and Sudarshan Chacha. He had set a rule that he would select only qualified children for his academy. He said he had limited seats, so he would only select those girls who already had potential. A rough diamond can be polished into a beautiful jewel, but a pebble cannot be turned into a diamond.

On the other hand, Lakhaniya and Baby were preparing for the state team. While practicing with the players on the state team, they didn't find anyone who posed a significant challenge to them.

One day, while practicing, Lakhaniya told Baby that the preparation they were doing at the sports hostel felt very easy. "Do you feel the same way?"

Baby replied, "That's because we were working for our livelihood, doing household chores, and preparing all in one day. There was a lot to do and little time, so everything was difficult. Now, we only have to think about playing; we don't have to worry about earning or home. Even after dedicating a lot of time to the game, we still have time left."

Lakhaniya agreed but had one complaint: she had come to the sports hostel thinking she would face tough competitors, but that wasn't the case. Most of the female runners were not able to compete with Lakhaniya and Baby. Because of this, their status on the state team was becoming like stars. They started to feel that they could easily handle all future competitions as well. This thought was gradually developing in them, that they had come through such harsh conditions that now, in the state team, there were no players who could keep up with them in practice.

In Manoj's world, everything was going well. New players had started practicing in the village. Everything was happening just as Manoj wanted. One night, Gudiya and Manoj were talking. Manoj was saying that kids from the surrounding areas were coming to the sports academy. Slowly, this entire region would become a sports hub. Exceptional players could emerge from here.

Gudiya was happy with Manoj's happiness; their baby's health had also improved, and she was healthy. A year had passed since her birth, and she was being raised well. Manoj had closed his grocery store and was now fully dedicated to the sports academy.

Time was passing. Everything was normal. When a person rises above the struggle for livelihood and existence, the next thing they desire most is respect and love. Every individual wants someone to pay attention to them, listen to their wounds, and declare them the hero of their story. Everyone keeps searching for such a person.

In the sports hostel, both girls were also going through this phase. In fact, a young man had entered Lakhaniya's life; he was also a state-level player in the sports hostel. They used to hang out together and practice together. Baby knew all about it and was happy that something good was happening in Lakhaniya's life. Now, evenings and mornings were passing like this. The boy's name was Rakesh. Rakesh's friends wanted to connect with Baby, but she didn't find anyone appealing and ignored them. Baby had asked Lakhaniya several times if there was anything serious between her and Rakesh, but Lakhaniya would laugh it off and say it was just an acquaintance.

Once, Baby teasingly said that when their acquaintance turns into a relationship, she should let her know. Lakhaniya laughed.

When Lakhaniya and Baby went to practice, Rakesh would also come there. Baby would step aside to give them some time together. Gradually, Lakhaniya became accustomed to feeling restless when she wasn't with Rakesh. Her mind was always occupied with thoughts of him. When Rakesh wasn't around, she would call him over. This new experience was adding a different dimension to both girls' lives.

One day, Lakhaniya came to Baby.

Lakhaniya: "Listen, I'm very happy today."

Baby had just returned from practice and was taking off her shoes.

Baby: "What happened?"

Lakhaniya: "Today, Rakesh told me that he loves me."

Baby: "Oh, he loves you? What was the need to say that? It was obvious to everyone."

Lakhaniya: "Oh, silly, it's very important to say it. Now it's confirmed. Before, it was just an assumption from both sides, but now it's a decision."

Baby: "Oh, so the decision is made...," and both started laughing.

There's a significant principle of love that everyone doesn't understand: love brings concentration, and if it doesn't provide the power to focus on a goal, then it's not love; it's something else. One day, after having a meal in the mess, Baby returned to the hostel room and saw Lakhaniya sobbing on her bed. The room was dark. She went to Lakhaniya and asked.

Baby: "What happened? You didn't even come for dinner."

Lakhaniya: "I just didn't feel like it."

Baby: "Did something happen?"

Saying this, Baby turned on the light and removed the blanket from Lakhaniya. Lakhaniya was crying. Then Lakhaniya told Baby that she had a terrible fight with Rakesh and had cut all ties with him from today.

Baby: "Oh, what happened?"

Lakhaniya: "Rakesh is just pretending; he meets me only when he needs something, talks only on his terms, and when I need him, he either disappears or makes some excuse. Why should I be the one to sacrifice to keep this relationship going?"

Baby: "But when you let go of him, he will be able to do his work. You either spend time with him or are on basic phone calls with him. When will he do his work?"

Lakhaniya: "Can any relationship survive without understanding each other?"

Baby: "But someone has to do their work."

Lakhaniya: "You won't understand; only those who burn in the fire know the pain. You have no idea."

Baby: "Yes, I don't know, but I don't think it's right for you to make such a terrible decision that it's all over."

Lakhaniya and Baby spent that entire night talking about Rakesh. The result was that both didn't wake up early in the morning and missed practice. Their trainer at the sports hostel scolded them that this way, training wouldn't work.

In the evening, when Lakhaniya and Baby went to practice, Rakesh arrived shortly after. Rakesh stepped forward to talk to Lakhaniya, but Baby interjected.

Baby: "Talk to me first; she won't talk to you."

Rakesh: "Baby, you're still a baby, don't act like a mother. Let me talk to Lakhaniya."

Hearing Rakesh's line, Rakesh's friends who had come with him started laughing. Lakhaniya chuckled slightly, while Baby felt shy.

Baby quickly replied, "Don't mess with me."

Seeing things escalate, Lakhaniya interjected, "Yes, go ahead, what do you want to say?"

After a while, the atmosphere changed. Rakesh presented such an apology to Lakhaniya that late at night, Lakhaniya and Rakesh returned from outside the sports hostel eating ice cream and humming a tune.

As they entered the room, Baby said, "Yesterday, you were acting like a fierce warrior, saying you wouldn't talk to Rakesh and that the whole relationship was over, and today you're back from having ice cream with him."

Lakhaniya replied, "You too were supposed to become a mother, but you came back after having ice cream."

From then on, it became a routine that whenever Lakhaniya and Rakesh had a fight, Baby would mediate. There is a certain pleasure in mediation, and this pleasure increases when one gets to mediate between lovers. There are many reasons for this pleasure; one reason is that the mediator is upholding the loyalty of friendship.

The second is that it brings a cool breeze into the empty space of love in their hearts, which they receive as a result of this mediation. Baby had also become accustomed to this cool breeze. But there are rules for achieving goals, and one of the hardest rules is to maintain concentration. Now, when the heart is absorbed in the drama of love and mediation, how can one maintain focus for achieving their goal?

Lakhaniya and Baby had started preparing for the National Games and were supposed to represent the state team. However, the problem was that their hard work wasn't quite up to par; they lacked the kind of training that Manoj was giving to them, and the trainer was not showing much interest. He had his own agenda and was working according to it while drawing a government salary. Lakhaniya's love life was also becoming very complicated, and she started spending most of her time with Rakesh.

Baby's time was increasingly consumed by handling various issues between Lakhaniya and her boyfriend. Excessive self-confidence is also an illusion that weakens the ability to sense challenges. Often, a person feels that if they have triumphed during the toughest times of their life, then subsequent weaker breezes won't affect them; they believe they are now more capable than before. But this excessive self-confidence weakens their preparation. This overconfidence was also taking root in the hearts of Lakhaniya and Baby; they had won so far without any issues, and they thought they would continue to win in the future.

# Chapter 21

The atmosphere of the village had changed, and both girls were feeling the shift in the air. Success boosts morale, which is why one starts feeling positive changes even in places where they have suffered for years. The national competition at the sports college was three months away, and both girls had come to the village during the ten-day Diwali holidays to finalize their preparations.

Manoj was excited by the news of both girls returning to the village. He called them to meet him. When the girls returned, they were astonished to see the sports academy started by Manoj and how well he had organized the training in the village. The number of girls coming to the sports academy for training had increased significantly. Manoj told both girls that while they were on holiday, they should come regularly to practice at the academy. This would not only inspire new girls to prepare but also ensure that Lakhaniya and Baby's practice didn't fall behind.

Both girls started coming to the academy every day based on Manoj's suggestion. Everything went smoothly for the first two or three days. Then one day, Manoj called Baby and asked from where Lakhaniya had gotten her mobile phone. This was a time when the whole world was rapidly moving from basic phones to mobiles. In around 2003, affluent people were starting to own mobile phones. So it was surprising to Manoj that Lakhaniya had a mobile phone, and an even bigger question was why she was so busy on it. Who pays the expensive mobile bills, and if she's always busy on the phone, when will she practice? If she's at the ground to practice, she should focus on that.

Baby quickly caught on to the situation and managed it by explaining, "Bhaiya, forms for the National competition are being filled out at the sports college. We both came here for the holidays, so Lakhaniya is talking to another player from the college to fill out our forms. That's why she keeps getting calls." The mobile phone belonged to a teammate from the sports college who had forgotten it in his room while going home for the holidays and had asked them to use it and return it after this break.

Manoj said, "Oh, that's the case, then it's fine. Just make sure there's no mistake in filling out the forms; otherwise, that guy might send them incorrectly, which could lead to issues later."

Baby replied, "That's why Lakhaniya is making sure to fill everything out correctly by herself."

Manoj said, "But there will be a holiday too..."

Baby responded, "Yes, she's just filling out the forms now. As soon as we leave here, we'll check, sign, and submit the forms, which will save our time in the process."

Chandan, who was standing there, remarked, "The girls have become quite knowledgeable after going to the city." Manoj nodded in agreement. Meanwhile, Lakhaniya was still on the phone.

After a while, when Lakhaniya joined them, Baby told her that Manoj was asking where she had been so busy on the phone. Lakhaniya asked what Baby had replied, and Baby narrated the excuse she had given.

Lakhaniya sighed; she worried that Baby might have inadvertently mentioned Rakesh to Manoj. But this matter didn't end there. Lakhaniya could be seen walking in the village streets under trees or in the fields and she is always visible on her mobile phone.

One day, Manoj told Chandan at the ground, "There's been a big change in Lakhaniya and Baby's demeanor. They're on the phone a lot." Chandan had seemingly been waiting for Manoj to say that so he could express his thoughts.

Chandan said, "They've caught the city vibe. If you give a poor person a bath, apply perfume, and make them wear expensive clothes, they might not even recognize themselves for days. Manoj replied, "What riddle are you posing?"

Chandan responded, "It's not a riddle; these two girls have gotten more than their worth. Last night, we saw Lakhaniya and Baby sitting behind the village in the woods at ten o'clock. They were chatting on the phone at the post where the animals are tied up behind their houses. Then, when I went to feed the buffalo at four in the morning, I saw them still talking on the phone while lying on the cot. I didn't say anything, just listened and left. This girl had been awake all night."

Manoj listened quietly. Lakhaniya was still on the phone. Suddenly, Manoj called out to Lakhaniya and Baby. The two girls came over, and Manoj told them to get ready to run and not to talk to anyone on the phone anymore. The girls didn't understand what had suddenly happened, but they complied with Manoj's instruction and got ready to run. Manoj had instructed them to do various exercises and go for a sprint race with some new girls coming to academy.

When the race ended, as always, Baby and Lakhaniya were in the lead. Baby came in first, and Lakhaniya second. Lakhaniya laughed, and Baby smiled, thinking that no one could defeat them today either.

Both girls approached Manoj, but his demeanor was different. He said, "I was watching the race, and even though you both won today, the difference between your time and the third-place girl wasn't much. It doesn't look good for state-level players, who have continuously won record races, to win by such a small margin against a novice runner." Manoj was not ready to end the conversation there.

Manoj continued, "Your speed, timing, and stamina have all diminished. Moreover, Baby's timing has improved compared to yours, Lakhaniya, while you were better than Baby in shorter races. In just a few races and a little exercise, fatigue has overwhelmed both of you. If this continues, you'll be dropped not only from the national team but also from the state team."

The two girls had been silently listening so far. But they were not liking Manoj's bitter words. Manoj continued, "It seems your heads are in the clouds. Don't forget how hard you worked to get here. Those who respect their struggle don't slack in their efforts; instead, they work even harder as they move toward their goals. But your attitudes are entirely different. All your bravado will fade away, and whatever heroine you think you are will come to an end."

Manoj kept grumbling, and after a while, Chandan came over and told the girls to go home. He even stopped the practice for all the other girls that day. Once everyone had left, Chandan told Manoj that scolding them was necessary. "It's not just about letting the kite fly high; you also need to pull it back at times."

On the other hand, Lakhaniya and Baby were very upset about this incident. Lakhaniya's ego had been hurt. After becoming a superstar athlete, hardly anyone had spoken to her like that. Baby acknowledged that there were shortcomings in both of them. "Manoj Bhaiya wasn't wrong," she said. But Lakhaniya did not agree with Baby's point and remained silent, feeling that the entire situation had arisen because she had been on her phone. If she spoke against Manoj Bhaiya, Baby would blame her.

Lakhaniya was seething inside. Ego is poisonous; as soon as it enters you, it corrupts your ability to differentiate between friends and foes. That night, after dinner, Lakhaniya called Rakesh and recounted the entire incident in detail. Girls who chat with their boyfriends on the phone do so with great pleasure; it brings them peace. They like boys who listen to them, and they particularly love those who defend them when they're wrong. Rakesh was familiar with this deep habit of girls and, like a clever boy, played his cards right, placing all the blame on Manoj Bhaiya.

Rakesh had already heard lengthy tales about Manoj's role in Lakhaniya and Baby's lives. He had long been looking for an opportunity to diminish Manoj's importance, and this could not have been a better opportunity. Rakesh said, "Look, Lakhaniya, don't take this the wrong way. Although Manoj ji helped you both a lot, he didn't do it just for you. He did it for himself as well. He was defeated in life, running a small shop, not having a government job, with debts looming over him. He took a gamble on you both to improve his own life. Today, he runs a sports academy in the village in your names, has cleared all his debts, is making money, and is buying a car. He's giving nothing to both of you. If you two were partners, you would have had to share the income, but he sees you both as his disciples, as his goddaughters."

Lakhaniya interjected, "The father is Harduram, not him." Rakesh replied, "No, you fool, I'm talking about a godfather, not just a father. The godfather is greater than the father. A father only gives birth, while a godfather creates an identity. But Manoj is not your godfather; you both are his godfathers. He could only do this because he met players like you. If he hadn't found players like you, could he have even dreamed of running a sports academy in the village or riding in a car?"

Lakhaniya nodded in agreement. "That's true."

Rakesh continued, "You both are state-level players today not because of anyone's favor but because of your passion and hard work, and when you win nationally tomorrow, it will be on your own merit, not relying on someone like Manoj. You create your own path, and you've proven that. As much as Manoj has helped you, you've repaid him tenfold, so he has no right to speak to you like that. I don't like it at all. Manoj is a cunning, sly man; I had a feeling he would turn out this way. Otherwise, why would anyone help so much without any greed?"

Rakesh ignited a fire in Lakhaniya's heart that burned throughout the night. A girl may not heed her husband's words, but her lover's words are etched in stone. In the throes of love, a girl submerged in romance hears her lover's voice as that of God. The next morning, she shared everything that had happened with Baby. At first, Baby hesitated, but then she too began to feel that Rakesh was not entirely wrong. Seeing Baby agree with her only fueled Lakhaniya's spirit further.

The next day during training, Lakhaniya repeated the same antics. But today, her actions were not just disobedience but rebellion, meant to shatter the illusion of the godfather she had learned about the previous night from her omniscient lover. Baby was engrossed in practice today, initially trying to convince Lakhaniya not to create a scene. But in love, people become rebels, and today a rebel was set to storm Manoj's academy. Lakhaniya's actions sent Manoj's temper soaring.

Manoj called out to Lakhaniya again. She took her phone away from her ear and walked over to him.

Manoj said, "You're causing a scene again. If you're not focused on practice, go home. Don't set a bad example for others who are practicing. I understand that your career is going to be ruined, and you'll end up returning home to just scoop cow dung."

As soon as Manoj said this, Lakhaniya shot back, "Bhaiya, don't play the godfather too much."

The wrong things taught by a lover become quickly ingrained in the hearts of their girlfriends. The moment "godfather" slipped from Lakhaniya's lips, silence fell over the place, and everyone turned to look at Manoj and Lakhaniya. Baby was completely taken aback, unsure of what had just happened. "Bhaiya, don't play the godfather too much. Whether our careers succeed or fail is in our hands. You have a misunderstanding that you've made Lakhaniya and Baby into athletes. If you made us athletes, it was for yourself, for this sports academy, to make money; otherwise, you were swatting flies at a grocery store. No one was there to ask about you."

Chandan interrupted, "Hey girl, shut up, what nonsense are you talking? Forgetting all favors, you're showing your true colors. The effects of your lineage don't fade away so easily."

Manoj stood there silently.

Chandan's interjection and caste-based comment ignited Baby's anger too.

Baby defended Lakhaniya, saying, "Why should we remain silent, and what color of caste have we shown? We've worked hard and bled to reach this point. There's no favor from anyone, and what Lakhaniya said isn't wrong. If someone taught us to play, there was a benefit for them too."

Chandan replied, "Wow, this is how you repay favors."

Baby and Lakhaniya spoke in unison, "What favor? Whatever you did, you did it for yourself; we were merely a means for you. If we weren't here, ask yourself if you could have won.The fire within us has led us to victory. Your contribution was in providing training, but when success came, you shared the credit too."

Manoj quietly walked away. Today, this entire spectacle had unfolded in front of everyone. All the girls who had come to the academy with Chandan had witnessed and heard everything.Manoj was very upset about the incident. It is undoubtedly painful when people misinterpret devotion and loyalty, leveling all kinds of baseless accusations. But it becomes a tragedy when the accusations come from those to whom you were loyal and dedicated.

Manoj was hurt by the argument with the girls. Chandan stated that it was a caste issue. He explained to Manoj that he had created so much hype that these girls were now flying above his head. When someone who hasn't been fed becomes a king, they start kicking their father. Manoj was trying to avoid harboring any malice, but the girls' rude behavior in front of the entire academy was distressing. That night, as Manoj lay quietly on his cot, Gudia spoke to him.

Gudiya: I found out from Chandan Bhaiya what happened at the academy today. What the girls did was definitely wrong. But don't harbor any resentment in your heart. If you think about it, the girls said what your opponents probably think about you.

Manoj: I'm not holding any resentment. I understand that what I was doing had my own interests at heart, but I'm saddened that the hard work I put in for a dream is now being ruined by these two girls. They can't comprehend the vision I have—a vision of change, of developing a sports culture in rural areas, empowering all common girls to explore opportunities in sports. I trusted Lakhaniya and Baby with that hope, and they've betrayed my deep trust. It's not about my gains or their gains; it's about losing sight of the entire goal we had set.

Gudiya: The girls may have spoken out of confusion; it's as simple as that.

Manoj: It's not just a simple matter; it's about a lack of discipline and focus. It's about not being able to understand that larger goal. When you are a forerunner of a dream, it is your moral responsibility to ensure that dream doesn't get destroyed. People may die, but they leave behind work that keeps the dream alive, that keeps the movement for change going, that leads to improvements in circumstances.

Gudiya: You're speaking like a revolutionary. Not everyone can stay focused all the time; they've been preparing for a long time, winning many races. It's essential to enjoy the victory too; they are human beings. There's a world beyond win and loss, and those girls want to exist in that world as well. Sometimes a break is necessary; otherwise, a person can't prepare for new goals. They might just be taking such a break, and you see it as a lack of focus. You want them to run continuously without taking a breath and keep winning.

Manoj: Why are you defending them?

Gudiya: Because you're blowing this out of proportion; it's not such a big deal. Both are young girls; a little leniency in focus can be lovingly explained. Give them some time; they'll find their way back.

Manoj: Do you think I don't know all this? But what those two did was a lack of discipline, and that tells me there's been a significant deviation from the goal.

Gudiya: Even if there's been a deviation, how will you stop them? Will they stop just because you explain it to them? Each person learns from their experiences, not from others' experiences.

Manoj: It's foolish to put your hand in the fire to know it burns; learning from others' experiences is essential.

Gudiya fell silent at Manoj's statement. But Manoj was also secretly acknowledging that Gudiya was right and that tying the girls down with excessive discipline would only worsen the situation rather than improve it. Manoj turned over and lay down. The fact was that the harmony between Manoj and the two girls was propelling them forward, and breaking that harmony was sure to cause harm. Manoj was very irritated by the accusation that he had used the girls' talent and ability for his benefit, and that was the only thing that was making him restless. Manoj believed he was pursuing a goal of social change, and establishing a sports academy aimed at creating a sports environment for girls in the village, not for developing income sources for him. If personal gain was the goal, why would he take on so much trouble and debt with so many efforts?

After all, how could someone accept their honest efforts as a selfish plan? Gudiya believed the girls were inexperienced and that Manoj should explain things to them lovingly once. Manoj agreed with Gudiya's point, but he knew that doing so wouldn't lead them to any destination. On the other hand, after such a contradiction arose between both sides, moving forward and discussing anything with the girls would feel like crushing his self-respect. Doing so would prove him wrong and the girls right, showing that everything Manoj did was solely for his financial benefit.

# Chapter 22

If there's anything the most powerful in the world, it's time, and what makes time powerful is its rule of not stopping. Time doesn't stop for anyone; it keeps moving forward, whether it's a mountain of sorrow or a storm of celebration. Time doesn't grant privileges to anyone—be it God, man, or beast.

A month had passed since the girls returned to the sports hostel. Manoj was busy training the athletes who came to his academy. He wanted to move forward without harboring any resentment in his heart. Commitment to a goal doesn't leave time for resentment. One day, Manoj was invited as a guest to the annual sports ceremony at his tehsil's college. That college belonged to a locally influential family, and at that time, the sitting MLA and a minister in the state government were also from that family. Impressed by Manoj's work, the minister himself called Manoj and requested him to attend the college's annual sports program, where there would also be discussions about the development of sports.

Manoj wasn't keen on attending such programs. He believed these events were merely formalities and a waste of time.. After thinking overnight, two thoughts crossed Manoj's mind. First, he thought that maybe people are becoming aware of sports, and by attending this program, he might meet some serious participants. Second, living in water and provoking a crocodile is always harmful, so there was no question of not attending the minister's program.

Finally, on the day of the event, Manoj reached there. Special arrangements were made for him to sit on stage. Ranveer was also sitting on that same stage. When Ranveer and Manoj saw each other, they smiled. Ranveer thought that Manoj's stature was rising so quickly that he was sharing the stage with a minister while still managing a grocery store, while it took him years and years of flattery to gain the same recognition.

Just as the annual sports ceremony began on stage, the minister received a call. After that call, the minister instructed his PA to call the District Magistrate (DM). The PA informed that the DM had just joined the day before and might not know about the issue the minister wanted to discuss. The minister ordered the PA to call DM. The PA called the DM and handed the phone to the minister.

The DM answered on the other end, "Sir, greetings."

Minister: "I've received information that you joined here yesterday."

DM: "Yes, sir, I joined yesterday evening."

Minister: "As it happens, the Honorable Chief Minister has appointed us as the minister in charge of your district, and we need to oversee all development work. We should hold a review meeting, so please call a coordination meeting with all district officials and public representatives today evening. We'll conduct this meeting today and I'll leave for the capital tomorrow morning."

DM: "Sir, I'll inform everyone about the meeting. Whatever orders you give, we'll prepare accordingly."

Minister: "One more thing: if there's any report on the major schemes, please show it to me before the meeting."

DM: "Sir, my PA informed me this morning that this meeting could be organized today evening, so I've already set my staff to prepare the report. It should be ready in the next two hours."

Minister: "Okay, please come to me with the report."

Saying this, the minister hung up. The PA asked the minister why he had called the DM personally when they would be at this program for two to three hours.

Minister: "This is our district; we get votes here, so it's essential to tighten the DM's bolts."

The PA understood the hint and quietly stepped back.

After a while, the activities at the sports ceremony concluded, and after the certificate distribution, it was time for the guests' speeches. All the guests were seated on the stage. Manoj was called to express his thoughts. As soon as Manoj reached the stage, the venue erupted with applause. Manoj had carved out a heroic image in that area. When a person builds a good image, many people start feeling jealousy for no reason because they couldn't achieve the same. Ranveer had never liked Manoj since childhood, and now his envy was eating him up, but he couldn't do anything against the minister. The minister had placed Manoj on a pedestal as a guest. Just as Manoj began to speak, several district administration vehicles arrived and came to a stop at the venue, with the DM's car leading the way.

In small areas, the position of the District Magistrate (DM) is very significant. Even though he is a bureaucrat in independent India, he has been given a status akin to that of a master.

Manoj was about to start speaking from the stage when the DM arrived. The DM was none other than Pooja. As she climbed the stairs, she was taken aback to see Manoj. She couldn't believe she was meeting him like this. On the other hand, Manoj was also surprised that fate had brought them face to face once again. The minister, seeing Pooja, asked her to sit on the chair beside him. The DM's guard stood back. Meanwhile, the announcer informed the audience and players about the DM's arrival through the microphone.

Announcer: "Friends, we have with us the District Magistrate of this district, Ms. Pooja Shriprakash. She took charge of this district just yesterday. Let's all welcome Madam."

Pooja was welcomed with thunderous applause.

Announcer: "Now, I would like to request Mr. Manoj to continue his speech and share his experiences with the young athletes. The way Mr. Manoj has played a role in preparing the athletes is inspiring for all of us, and we believe that in the coming years, this tehsil will shine across the country, and many exceptional athletes will emerge."

The applause echoed again, and Manoj took the microphone once more.

Manoj: "Friends, on this occasion, I welcome the honorable Minister, the District Magistrate, other distinguished guests, and all of you present here. I will present my thoughts; it might be a bit lengthy, but it's important for your future because I wouldn't want you to make the same mistakes I did. Learning from others' experiences and recognizing the thorns in your paths is essential, and I hope you understand that. I do not want to limit my discussion to sports alone. Today's youth primarily thinks about employment because they know that employment is what enables them to support themselves and easily fulfill their family responsibilities. It allows them to establish a place in society, and this is a fundamental question.

But now the question arises: can playing sports lead to a career that eliminates the crises of livelihood, identity, and sustenance? My answer is that sports can certainly be such a path where an individual can achieve this milestone, but every path has its own challenges, its own struggles, and every path requires honesty, hard work, dedication, and discipline. If you lack these qualities, you will not succeed on any path you take. The same rules apply in the world of sports.

Another issue is that our society does not give enough importance to sports; more importance is given to employment. Government jobs are considered so significant that they are thought to be a means of elevating generations. But friends, this is a time for change. In the next twenty to thirty years, the way our society thinks will change significantly, and those who can do something new during this period will set inspirational examples in society."

Hearing Manoj's inspiring words, the venue erupted in applause.

Manoj continued speaking. "Change in life is a very necessary process. Some people even leave government jobs, which indicates that satisfaction is not achieved here either. In such a case, if you are not getting a government job, pursue what you are passionate about and where you can find employment. Everyone has some quality that makes them special; identify that quality, hone it, and establish your place.

Do not be afraid of change; make significant efforts through legitimate means in society because life is very short. Develop new ideas and work on them. Those who work on new ideas are often ridiculed, but when someone works on a new idea and gains recognition, others aspire to work for them rather than creating their own new ideas.

Invest and earn profits, and with those profits, create new employment opportunities and new creative teams. In many fields, there is a mentality of embezzlement associated with investment. If such a mindset prevails, not only will investments fail, but new investors will also not come forward, and innovation will come to a halt.

This is a major reason for the lack of development in many sectors. Stop ridiculing those who develop new ideas; instead, try to learn from them. If some new idea has emerged in another state or city, try to adapt and develop it in your local conditions. Do not mock those who are attempting something new just for the sake of conformity. To achieve something great, an entrepreneurial environment must be created.

With a narrow-minded thought that we are the only capable ones while everyone else is foolish, no one can progress. In areas where there are good opportunities for entrepreneurship, people make minimal attempts for government jobs. In places where there is maximum pursuit of government jobs, it indicates that better alternative opportunities are lacking. Therefore, collective efforts are needed for better alternative opportunities.

Look, we live in a feudal society; everyone seems to understand only the language of authority. That might be why people want to enter civil services even after doing IIT or AIIMS. This is not our priority but rather a societal priority shaped by our family's economic and social conditions. We may be writers at heart but aspire to be police officers. We may be scientists inside, yet we qualify for SSC and become accountants. The result is that we are neither happy ourselves nor with society. We are becoming complacent, and we are making too many compromises.

The most intellectually capable youth in India is wasting their initial ten years preparing for government jobs. If someone spends ten years preparing for a job in an average lifespan of sixty years, they are committing a sin against their life. But will anyone accept my words universally? Yet the reality is, for those who qualify, it's fine, but what about those who do not? A chaotic life filled with despair awaits them. I have come to understand this myself because I have stumbled along this path. Therefore, my advice is that our efforts should be focused on knowing ourselves and understanding what we truly want so that societal and familial preferences do not overpower us."

Silence enveloped the assembly, and people were eager not to miss a single word of Manoj's speech.

Manoj then said, "Economic and social conditions can be your adversaries. But have faith in yourself; there is no remedy other than self-belief. Recognize yourself, assess your capabilities, determine your priorities, and then struggle. I assure you, if you align your attitude and your capabilities, no one will be able to hold back your success. However, if you create a disparity between your attitude and capabilities, you will not only harm society but also turn this invaluable human life into a book of compromises.

A person who has a mindset of earning a lot of money, if they become a government officer, what will they do? You can understand that. They will neither be honest about their work nor with their mindset. Yes, if they become a businessman instead, their mindset will be satisfied, and they will contribute to society by providing jobs to ten others. Development of the nation does not happen through jobs; only the individual benefits from jobs. The development of a country happens through entrepreneurship, and this very simple fact is often overlooked by many policy experts.

When a person from a village secures a job, it brings economic development to them and their family, while entrepreneurship begins to lead to the economic development of multiple individuals and their families. It has to be determined what is more effective: giving everyone jobs without entrepreneurship is also not feasible.

So, seek yourself, understand yourself...

There is no greater struggle than this, and there is no greater success than this. If our education does not allow us to explore ourselves and fails to instill faith in us to do something creative, then believe me, in this world where money is worshipped, you are being rendered helpless, like a person trapped in the illusion of labor, dreaming of more wages, more comfort, more amenities, and more security. But perhaps a human being should realize that true security lies only in death. Therefore, there will certainly be no end to their exploration, and there will be no end to their thoughts."

A strong background gives more freedom and options in choosing the right job. A laborer's son will surely think of filling his stomach first before dreaming of becoming an athlete, even if there's an Olympic champion within him. Those who have money can afford to ruin ten jobs and still have the capacity to try something new in the next one. Most people, even after recognizing their inner fire, get so caught up in the struggle for daily bread that they eventually give up their interests.

The result is that they cannot perform at their best. To pursue what one desires, most people have to work under poor conditions, make compromises, and flatter inferior people. But all this is part of life's lessons; the understanding that develops in one's personality from this experience cannot be found in books. The real profound knowledge comes from here. However, this knowledge can be very painful, continuously tormenting the soul. Therefore, keep doing what you are doing for your livelihood while also progressing toward your goals; one day will surely come when the time will be yours, and the opportunity will be yours. At that moment, do not hesitate to follow your heart. Better than unemployment, take any job you get and, while working, prepare a way to do what you truly enjoy.

Greetings, thank you, Jai Siyaram.

With these words from Manoj, his address concluded, and the venue echoed with applause for several minutes. The ministers, including Ranveer, on stage were astonished. Even Pooja was feeling the resonance of Manoj's words in surprise. She was mesmerized to see this side of Manoj.

After the event, the minister praised Manoj heartily and introduced him to Pooja, informing her that Manoj had also gone to Delhi to prepare for UPSC and had reached the interview stage.

Pooja quietly absorbed this information. Neither Manoj nor Pooja let anyone feel that they knew each other. There was no initiation from either side; they both greeted each other formally and moved on.

After the event, Manoj was returning to his village in a tempo. Throughout the journey, he was contemplating how his past had come back to him. Pooja occupied his thoughts; seeing a first love again leaves one in a daze, and that was the case for Manoj. If time is the most powerful force in the world, then love is that feeling that successfully maintains its existence even beyond time. Manoj knew that a lot of time had passed, but his heart still leaned towards Pooja. He felt very happy seeing Pooja as a district magistrate, recalling that he had dreamed of both of them becoming officers as husband and wife while preparing together. Although the dream didn't materialize, Pooja had become just the kind of officer he envisioned in his dreams. He felt a sense of happiness about this.

The fragrance of first love is so intense that it lingers in your mind for years. Whenever it rains, when moods change, or when the weather is pleasant, this fragrance blossoms and fills the entire being with joy. Today, Manoj was experiencing that joy. As soon as he entered his home, when Gudiya greeted him, thoughts of Pooja left his mind. That night, on the terrace under the moonlight, Chandan was telling Manoj that his speech had caused quite a stir. Ranveer had told Chandan that Manoj could become a leader; he was running a sports academy. Manoj laughed at Ranveer's statement.

Chandan said, "Yeah, I didn't believe it at first either."

Manoj replied, "It's a big deal when those who don't like you praise you; it means there's something in you."

Chandan said, "No, it's not just that; my brother is blunt."

Both laughed.

Chandan added, "Hey, did you hear? The new DM was also there today. I've heard she's very beautiful."

Manoj replied, "Yes, she was; she is beautiful."

Chandan continued, "She's a very sharp officer; she made life miserable for all the troublemakers in her last district where she was the SDM."

Manoj said, "Yes, I know; she's stubborn; she can make life miserable."

Chandan asked, "How do you know?"

Manoj replied, "I know her from my days in Delhi."

Chandan exclaimed, "Wow, that's impressive; now you're the star, and everyone must have learned about it at the program today."

Manoj said, "Star? She's the DM; I'm not. Besides, none of us mentioned that we were previously acquainted at the event."

Chandan asked, "Why not?"

Manoj explained, "Look, Chandan, understand this rule: If a friend or acquaintance of yours achieves a significant position, they will determine the level of connection, they want to maintain with you."

# Chapter 23

Meanwhile, upon returning to the sports hostel, there was no improvement in the practice of either girl. Lakhaniya and Baby generally assumed that they weren't at fault in their clash with Manoj. Thus, they felt no remorse. However, during this time, something new and surprising had happened. Rakesh was keeping an excessive distance from Lakhaniya, and she was worried about this sudden change in his behavior. Lakhaniya spent all her time wondering why Rakesh was acting this way, while Baby was busy comforting her. Rakesh wasn't meeting them or even staying in touch over the phone.

Lakhaniya and Baby were sitting in their room talking. Lakhaniya couldn't understand why there was such a change in Rakesh's behavior.

Baby asked, "Tell me, did something happen between you and Rakesh?"

Lakhaniya asked, "What do you mean?"

Baby gestured, and Lakhaniya understood.

Lakhaniya replied, "Oh no, he tried hard to trap me, but I know what boys want."

Baby said, "So nothing happened?"

Lakhaniya responded, "Only as much as I wanted; the rest is his business."

Baby added, "But think, if you do all this before marriage, boys easily run away. They get what they want and also doubt that if she can do this with me, she can do it with anyone. Maybe she has done it with someone before, so she's not material to become a wife."

Lakhaniya snapped, "Your thinking is getting too excessive."

Baby replied, "Boys are very cunning; they will try to hit on you and then clean their faces, but they will dig into a girl's past."

Lakhaniya got irritated, "I'm already stressed, and you keep talking nonsense."

After a while, both decided to contact Rakesh's friends to find out what was going on with him, hoping to gain some insight. After speaking with many of Rakesh's friends, they discovered that he had gone home for several days, but they didn't know much else.Weeks were passing, and Rakesh's situation was not resolving. The National Games were approaching. Lakhaniya was unable to find mental stability.

The entire preparation was reliant on God's will. During practice, her body might have been running, but her mind was elsewhere. To win, it's essential for the body and mind to be in sync. Yet, Lakhaniya and Baby remained confident that they would win at the National Games based on their own strength.

One day, Lakhaniya and Baby were out shopping when they spotted Rakesh. He was with a very beautiful girl. Rakesh and the girl were heading somewhere in the market.

By the time Lakhaniya and Baby crossed the street to reach Rakesh, he had already disappeared from sight. However, the truth was that Rakesh had noticed Lakhaniya and Baby following him.

That night, Lakhaniya called Rakesh, and he answered the phone. Initially, Lakhaniya scolded Rakesh, but he did not admit to any wrongdoing. He told her to be patient because his father was very ill, and he had been preoccupied with his treatment, which was why he hadn't been able to answer Lakhaniya's calls.

Rakesh's voice, filled with pain and compassion, was proving to Lakhaniya that he was speaking the truth. But the question still remained: who was the girl with Rakesh that day? Rakesh claimed she was a girl from his family. He had sent some money home through her, and since he had run out of cash, she had come to give it to him. They had gone to the bank just to withdraw the money. Rakesh said that if there was still doubt, Lakhaniya could punish him in any way she wished. Lakhaniya had nothing more to say now. Rakesh was innocent, and he had proven it. He had mentioned that he would meet Lakhaniya soon after resolving all his family issues. In love, reassurances hold value, and Lakhaniya had trusted that assurance.

On the other hand, Manoj had returned to training the children at his academy after the girls had left. However, he was unhappy with the performance of the girls who were coming in for training. He often reiterated to Chandan that the new girls lacked the fire to win that Lakhaniya and Baby had.

Chandan: Why do you think these kids won't reach that level?

Manoj: I haven't seen the desire to win in any of them like I did in Lakhaniya and Baby. They view sports as an alternative; if they can't succeed elsewhere, they will pursue this, or if they achieve something, they will continue, otherwise they'll drop it.

Chandan: So, what should happen then?

Manoj: In a race, only those players who fight for life will win like kings; those who merely exist will only keep running, achieving nothing,

Chandan.: So we should choose such children from among them. That's possible, right?

Manoj: These are all children of the privileged. To have the hunger to win, one needs to experience pain and hardship. They need a wound in the mind to strive for victory. Here, there's none of that.

Chandan: Can one bring such a wound in the mind from within? After a long discussion to resolve this issue, Manoj concluded that finding a worthy guru is impossible for any disciple; hence, a worthy guru finds the right disciples themselves. With this thought, Manoj decided to organize a camp to select good girls.

Participants were required to share their family backgrounds, reasons for joining sports, and their strategies for winning, in addition to passing a physical test. It was also decided that the academy would bear the training costs for those girls who passed the test, and all participants were informed about this. Manoj and Chandan promoted the camp in far-off villages and areas to attract as many girls as possible.

After a few days, Manoj successfully organized the camp. The positive outcome was that he met several girls at the camp who could be polished into diamonds. Now, all of Manoj's hopes were pinned on these newly selected girls, as his experiences with Baby and Lakhaniya had been disappointing, and he did not want any further contact with them.

In the evening, Chandan came to meet Manoj and asked, "What do you see different in these children, brother? They all look the same to me; the previous ones were like this too." Manoj: Actually, these are the children who will only succeed in life if they win in races. I won't need to provide any additional motivation to teach them; the fire within them will inspire them, and I'll take care of the rest. That same fire was in Lakhaniya and Baby.

Chandan: So, these kids might end up like Baby and Lakhaniya tomorrow and say, "We did everything ourselves; what did you do?" Manoj laughed and replied, "That can happen, and it will happen. But that would be a misunderstanding. As long as fire is uncontrolled, it only causes destruction; only when it is controlled can it create something new. Learning control is essential; if it could come naturally, there would never be a need for teachers or gurus in the world."

# Chapter 24

It was afternoon, and Gudiya was hanging clothes at home while Manoj was fixing an old fan. Sweat was dripping from Manoj, but he was focused on repairing the fan. In middle-class families, men have to become handymen by trying to fix everything. If they don't, a significant part of their income goes toward repairs. The little girl was sleeping inside. Just then, a lot of police and villagers were seen moving outside.

Gudiya called out to Manoj, "Hey, listen! There's so much police and many villagers outside."
Manoj paused, asking, "What happened?"

Gudiya: "I don't know."

Manoj left the fan and, draping a towel over his sweaty vest, stepped out of the house. As soon as he stepped outside, he saw that everyone was passing in front of his house. Some police officers were present, and the village head was leading the group. As more people moved aside, Manoj spotted Pooja. Before he could think, the village head pointed towards Manoj and said to Pooja, "Madam, this is Manoj Babu, a very renowned coach. The children he trains play at the national level."

Pooja also paused upon seeing Manoj. The village head then said, "Manoj Babu, Madam is the Collector, and she came to inspect the village's primary school." Manoj joined his hands in greeting Pooja. She paused for a moment and accepted his greeting with folded hands.

Manoj thought Pooja would directly head to her government vehicle parked a short distance away outside the village. However, Pooja stayed there, gazing intently at Manoj. He felt momentarily flustered until Pooja spoke, "Manoj, how are you?" Hearing his name from

Pooja after so many years momentarily lost him in thought. Pooja repeated, "Manoj, how are you?"

Village Head: "Hey Manoj Babu, Madam is asking you something."
Manoj: "I'm fine, Pooja. It's great to see you here."

At that moment, everyone present froze, wondering what Manoj had just said to the Collector. He had responded using her name. Pooja quickly sensed the situation and managed it by saying, "Village Head, Manoj is my old friend. We studied together in Delhi, and it's fortunate that I got to meet him today while visiting the village."

Upon hearing this, the villagers were left astonished, and the village head exclaimed, "Wow, what a miracle!

A friend from Delhi meeting here in the village!"

Everyone laughed, but Manoj and Pooja remained completely silent, as if something deep within them was being suppressed.

Pooja continued, "Manoj, aren't you going to take me to your home?" Manoj snapped back to reality, saying, "Oh yes, of course! My home is right here. You are very welcome. Come, Pooja." Pooja went towards Manoj's house with her bodyguard.

Gudiya was watching from the ledge of her house and, seeing Manoj coming with everyone, she went inside. As soon as Manoj entered the house, he arranged for everyone to sit, but he felt a little hesitant since there wasn't enough seating for so many people. Just then, Pooja told her bodyguard to wait outside. She would meet Manoj's family and asked the steno to inform the BDO to reach Munirpur village for the further investigation.

The bodyguard and everyone else went outside.

Now there was complete solitude between Pooja and Manoj. A few moments passed without either of them saying anything. Pooja broke the silence, asking, "Is no one else at home?"

Manoj replied, "Oh yes, I forgot to mention. My wife is inside." Pooja asked, "Are you not going to introduce me?"

Manoj said, "You sit down; I will definitely introduce you." He went inside, where Gudiya was already waiting for him with questions.

Gudiya asked, "Who is this?"

Manoj replied, "She's the collector madam, here to meet you. She's familiar from our days in Delhi; she used to study with me there."

Gudiya said, "She's familiar from Delhi days, but you never mentioned it."

Manoj reassured her, "I will explain everything in detail later. She's here to meet you and is waiting outside. You should go and meet her."

Gudiya responded, "Okay, you go outside and talk; I'll bring some snacks."

Manoj stepped outside.

Pooja asked, "Where's your wife? She hasn't come to meet me."

Manoj answered, "She's coming."

Pooja inquired, "What about your sister Anju? Where is she?"

Manoj replied, "Anju got married. She lives in a nearby village."

Pooja then asked about his father, saying, "How is your father's health? I don't see him."

Manoj said, "Father passed away, Pooja. He died when I returned from Delhi."

Pooja was stunned for a moment.

She then asked, "Is that why you didn't come back to Delhi?"

Manoj, after a brief silence, said, "What could I do? Anju was alone; there was no one here."

Before Pooja could ask anything further, Gudiya came back with a glass of water and a plate of sweets.

Manoj introduced, "This is my wife, Gudiya."

Gudiya greeted Pooja. Pooja stood up and hugged Gudiya. Manoj watched them from a distance.

Pooja said, "I'm Pooja; I studied with Manoj in Delhi. I've been posted here in this district, so I came to check on things and unexpectedly met Manoj."

Gudiya replied, "Yes, he mentioned you. It's great that you came; it will make him happy. He has no friends here except for Chandan Bhaiya. Meeting you will remind him of our Delhi days."

Pooja agreed, "Yes, that's true. Come, sit with us."

Gudiya said, "No, I'll go get tea, and then we can sit together."

Pooja insisted, "I'm not here for tea; I came to meet you. Forget about tea; let's sit here." The three of them sat down.

Just then, they heard a baby crying from inside.

Gudiya said, "Who is it? The baby has woken up! I'll go check." She went inside, leaving Pooja and Manoj alone.

Manoj said, "She just turned one year old."

Pooja gazed at Manoj, who felt shy under her scrutiny. Pooja, regaining her composure, asked, "May I meet the baby?"

Manoj replied, "Yes, of course." He called Gudiya to bring the baby.

As soon as Pooja saw the baby, she picked her up, kissed her forehead, and placed four five-hundred-rupee notes in her lap.

Manoj exclaimed, "Pooja, why are you giving so much? There's no need for it."

Pooja, addressing Gudiya, said, "I came unexpectedly, and I didn't know I would meet you. Please don't refuse this; buy some clothes and toys for her on my behalf. The next time I come, I will bring more myself."

Gudiya said, "No, didi, please come again next time and give it then."

Pooja replied, "Next time, I will bring separate toys for my child; this is for this time."

Manoj interjected, "Pooja, that doesn't seem right."

Pooja scolded him, "Don't lecture me on what's right and what's not."

Pooja became emotional. Her eyes welled up, but she tried to compose herself. She then said, "Alright, I'll take my leave." To Gudiya, she said, "If you come to the city, please do visit me. Now that you've called me didi, you must come."

As she patted the baby's head, she started to leave the house. Manoj went to see her off while Gudiya stayed inside.

As they walked back, Pooja quietly said to Manoj, "Destiny plays strange tricks; I used to dream of coming to this house, but not as a daughter-in-law and a collector."

Manoj couldn't say anything; he felt a deep sorrow upon seeing Pooja's expression, but being in a public place, he kept his composure. Just then, seeing the collector coming out of the house, the bodyguard, other officials, the village head, and others arrived there.

Manoj folded his hands to greet Pooja.

Pooja looked at Manoj... Manoj couldn't meet her eyes, feeling as if he had done a great injustice to her. He hadn't anticipated that Pooja would meet him like this.

Moments later, everyone left, and when Manoj went inside, Gudiya was standing there.

Gudiya said, "The collector madam was very nice and friendly, showing so much affection towards us."

Manoj remained silent and didn't say anything. After a moment, he replied, "She's a big officer. Coming to our door and giving us such respect is a significant thing. People often forget their roots when they rise to greatness, but she remains the same as she was."

Gudiya nodded in agreement.

# Chapter 25

Both girls, wearing tracksuits and sports shoes, set off towards Rakesh's hostel. It was evening, and the sun was about to set. Upon reaching the hostel, Lakhnia called Rakesh's intercom from the reception, but he didn't pick up. Frustrated, Lakhnia asked another boy standing there about Rakesh, who informed her that Rakesh was standing at the back of the hostel with some other boys. When Lakhnia and Baby went around to the back, they saw Rakesh standing there smoking a cigarette with his friends. Just then, Lakhnia overheard their conversation.

Rakesh's friend said, "Bro, now there's a show! The father-in-law is the Joint Director of the Sports Authority. The future wife is an Assistant Professor. What else do you need? Your life is set, dude."

Rakesh took a long drag when another friend chimed in, "But what will you do about her?"

"Whom?" asked Rakesh.

"Oh, that Lakhnia."

Rakesh replied, "We'll handle her; giving her some attention is enough. In his entire life, he won't find such a fair, beautiful, and well-built girl again. Has he even looked at his own face?"

His friend said, "But you used to hang out with her."

Rakesh responded, "What should I do? When times are tough, one has to make do with whatever is available. If she gets too clingy, it'll become a problem. She's harboring dreams of a forced marriage. No caste, no looks, and no brains."

Lakhnia and Baby overheard all of this. Baby wanted to confront Rakesh, but Lakhnia stopped her and made her swear to quietly leave. The three boys continued their conversation. The two girls returned to their room silently. Sometimes problems seem to be over, but that's not the case; often, it's due to not understanding the situation correctly or ignoring the truth. This was a big shock for Lakhnia, and she didn't know what to do next. She had never expected to hear something like this.

Three days later, the National Games were held. Baby and Lakhnia also participated in the race, but what happened was what was bound to happen. Until then, it had been a record that Lakhnia and Baby won all the races. But for the first time, they didn't even make it under five in all the National competitions. This terrible defeat broke them. Everyone expected them to win, as they were destined to win. But this time, the story was different. Without practice, success doesn't come. For success, one needs continuous enthusiasm, courage, motivation, hard work, and discipline, but failure only requires one mistake. Lakhnia and Baby had made that mistake. Their image of being super girls was shattered. Sometimes, wrong decisions hit hard.

This happened to Lakhnia; the betrayal from Rakesh not only deeply hurt her but also led to their eviction from the state-level hostel after losing in the National Games. The biggest blow for Lakhnia was that she had fought with Manoj Bhaiya at the behest of a selfish and deceitful person like Rakesh. Baby's despair was at a different level. She suffered the consequences of bad company. Baby's loss was too much connected to Lakhnia's entanglement, resulting from a lack of concentration and discipline.

After this incident, Lakhnia was in shock, feeling as though she had lost everything after gaining it all. This is the hardest situation when you lose everything after having it all; you can't even be happy in your former worse state because you realize how much potential you had and how you fell back due to terrible mistakes.

Now Lakhnia and Baby were back to zero. Baby was still strong, but Lakhnia was unable to cope with the shock. Baby tried very hard to console her, but Lakhnia was so broken that she couldn't get a grip on herself. After losing in the National Games, there was a rule to vacate the state sports hostel before the next season, and it was now the last day for Lakhnia and Baby to vacate. Baby went to the bathroom, and when she returned to the room, she found Lakhnia missing. When Baby couldn't find Lakhnia, she panicked.

On the other hand, Lakhnia had come out quietly to buy something on the main road, but her mind was racing with thoughts, and she was oblivious to the traffic coming her way. She felt she was becoming the same Lakhnia who used to graze goats and sell vegetables, doing others' household chores. All these thoughts brought darkness before her eyes, and just then a truck came from the opposite direction, and the people around shouted. Lakhnia barely escaped; just as she was about to be hit, someone pulled her back.

Lakhnia turned around and saw it was Manoj. He had read about Baby and Lakhnia's defeat in the newspapers, and Baby had called him to explain everything. Manoj told Baby he would come and take them both, and until then, he wouldn't tell Lakhnia anything. Seeing Manoj, Lakhnia burst into tears and started apologizing. Manoj told her to pull herself together and said, "Lakhnia, life teaches this way. You must handle yourself; nothing happens either in your favor or against it.

Sometimes things depend on what intention you had and what you did based on that intention. No one is so perfect that they reach their destination without making mistakes. I have also made mistakes in my life."

When Manoj brought Lakhnia back to the hostel, Baby explained everything to him in detail. Manoj listened patiently to everything. He said it was essential to understand one thing: there will be mistakes in life because none of us are perfect. We all have some shortcomings.

The second thing is that big victories require losses because respect for victory comes from them. Your mistake has proven that even though you both have a natural talent for running, better than others, without patience until success, despair will soon surround you, and all your possibilities will vanish. Only fools expect everything to go their way. In ninety percent of cases, that doesn't happen. Continuous improvement is necessary.

Both girls agreed with Manoj's words. He said that when mistakes happen and everything goes wrong, one should throw away all despair and start anew, just like the first time. That's what gives energy. If you let old mistakes dominate you, that despair will prevent you from trying again. Lakhnia said, "But Bhaiya, I can't just forget everything suddenly."

Manoj replied, "The shortcomings within you may feel bad because you consider them important. To overcome that shortcoming, first stop seeing it as significant and try to improve it. As a person gets closer to success, the fear of failure increases fourfold. You must not let this fear dominate you because just thinking about losing significantly diminishes the chances of winning. If you can learn something new from every failure and loss, one day it makes you an expert in your field, and once you become an expert, any person rises above loss and victory."

The courage from Manoj's words infused Baby and Lakhnia with a new energy, and for the first time, they felt they could struggle through the circumstances and make their place again. That night, Baby, Lakhnia, and Manoj talked openly, and both girls resolved all their grievances with Manoj. Manoj, showing magnanimity, forgave both girls.

He told them that without discipline in life, no one can maintain consistent morale. To keep morale high, practice is essential, and discipline is necessary for practice. After that, Manoj told both girls that the next day they should take him to Rakesh and, if possible, find out when Rakesh would meet the girl he was going to marry.

The next day, Lakhnia gathered information from a boy at Rakesh's hostel, who didn't like Rakesh but still stayed with him. That boy told Lakhnia everything and also mentioned that Rakesh was going to meet that girl either today or tomorrow. Manoj then explained the plan to

Baby and Lakhnia. Initially, Lakhnia rejected the plan and said she wanted to forget all this and focus on practice back in the village.

Then Manoj said one thing: "You should definitely forget everything and make a fresh start. But sometimes, giving a lesson to someone who has wronged you can boost your own morale, and you should do that if necessary. In football, victory goes to the one who can score against the opponent while also defending their own goal. You cannot afford to let this match go to waste; Rakesh has started it by scoring one goal. Now you must at least score one goal to make the match a draw. You can rest assured; I will handle everything."

After Manoj's assurance, both girls gained confidence. According to the information received by Lakhaniya, at the appointed time, Manoj left with both girls to meet Rakesh along with Baby. Rakesh was sitting with his new girlfriend in a restaurant. The three of them arrived there.

Manoj told Lakhaniya, "When I say, slap Rakesh hard, and the slap should be so strong that it speaks for everything you want to say, so that you don't have to say anything at all."

Baby said, "Brother, do you think she can do it?"

Manoj replied, "Baby, sometimes treating the one who has hurt you can heal some wounds. This is that wound."

Rakesh and his future wife were sitting face to face at the table, taking turns eating the same ice cream, establishing their unity in love, when, as per Manoj's instruction, Lakhaniya went ahead and slapped the boy hard, stripping him of the last remnants of respect. Both girls exposed all of Rakesh's deceit in front of his new girlfriend and warned her that if she married such a boy, she would spend her life managing his affairs. When Rakesh tried to show some temper, Manoj tightened the situation.

After this, both girls came out of the restaurant with Manoj like winners, turning towards a new beginning. A calm after the storm now resided in Lakhaniya's heart. At that moment, both girls felt as if they were being reborn. After returning to the village, Manoj told Lakhaniya and Baby to completely forget the past and start practicing again.

"Before you can run, you need to learn to walk. Long jumps can cause injuries if you're not practiced. This lesson in life often teaches us to keep trying," he said. Both girls rejoined the practice after returning to the village. Manoj was full of enthusiasm again. This time, he wanted other girls who could play well to qualify at the state level. With Baby and Lakhaniya's return, his morale was even higher.

To boost their spirits, Manoj kept saying that they would qualify for the state again, and this time they would make it to the nationals. About three more months passed. One day, Pooja sent a message to Manoj saying that she wanted to come to his academy to see how he trained the girls. Manoj immediately agreed. A person in love can never refuse anything.

No one can defeat time, but true love has the quality of conquering it, living beyond time in the heart. Even though Pooja and Manoj's paths were now separate, Pooja still held a place in Manoj's heart, and perhaps something similar was true for Pooja as well.

Soon, Pooja was present at Manoj's academy. Manoj introduced all the girls to the Collector, and also introduced Baby and Lakhaniya to her. He even introduced Pooja to Chandan.

That evening, Pooja stayed at the academy to watch the training session. When the training was over and the girls left, Pooja and Manoj remained there. Pooja's guards and staff were a little distance away.

Pooja said, "I'm very happy for you; you have handled yourself so well. I had no idea what happened when you didn't return to Delhi. Some people said very negative things about you."

Manoj asked, "What negative things did they say?"

Pooja laughed and said, "Oh, forget it..."

Manoj continued, "They said he has become frustrated..."

Pooja replied, "In such situations, what else can people say? But you made a good comeback."

Manoj responded, "The comeback was very difficult, but it was the last resort."

Pooja added, "In life, those who achieve their goals on their own terms often find that things don't go as they planned. Life moves at its own pace. It has its own rules for turning and twisting, and whenever you think your life is going to be a straight line, it will turn quickly and not give you a chance to recover."

Manoj listened to Pooja.

He asked, "How's your job going? It must feel good; you always wanted to do this."

Pooja explained, "The success of young people passing exams like IAS or PCS is only personal success until they work impartially and sincerely for social change. Social problems should not be edited with prejudice, but transparently and creatively addressed. A thousand people come to get jobs; that's not success. So, cherishing the importance of getting a position or passing an exam not only harms you personally but also hinders the process of reforming the system and the spirit of public service."

Manoj commented, "You haven't changed at all; you still have that same spirit. I can see the same Pooja who stood on the terrace of that building in Delhi, debating various contemporary topics with me."

Pooja laughed, "But back then, there was more theory in life, and today it's all about practicalities. Principles are fading away."

Manoj remarked, "But you're still doing your job, right?"

Pooja responded, "I am working, but the practical challenges are entirely different. You can't do much most of the time; you can only remain a spectator. The system has its own pace, and if you try to speed it up or meddle with it, you have to be ready to face the consequences. If you understand this and accept it, then doing a job becomes very easy because it's an easy path, which is why most people choose it. Those who can't do that suffocate; they get caught between establishing ideals and practicalities."

Manoj continued to listen carefully to Pooja's every word. After becoming an IAS, IPS, PCS, or any other high-ranking officer, if you stop using public toilets, avoid going out on city streets filled with husbands and wives, stop using public transport like buses, tempos, autos, and rickshaws, and avoid traveling in general compartments of trains, then you will not understand the problems of ordinary people.

You will develop a sense of superiority, and you will become detached from the common people's problems. When the issues of the class you belong to are no longer your issues, how will you find solutions to them? You won't be able to—only continue building castles in the air under the pretence of solutions.

Then you will become an insensitive officer, disconnected from social change, only doing your job while focusing solely on enhancing the facilities available to you. Remember, those who think, "I just need to do my job," cannot bring about reform in the system, and those who want to make changes will have to pay a price. What that price is will vary based on different circumstances.

Manoj reflected, "Everything is so complex. We thought that when we became officers, control would be in our hands, and we could do everything as we wished. But as you explain, it seems that no matter what level a person reaches, the crisis of existence will always trap you in some competition or struggle."

Pooja suddenly says, "Oh, I almost forgot something in our conversation. I brought some books for you. I thought you liked reading, so I brought them."

Pooja calls for the books from her car and hands them to Manoj. Manoj happily accepts the books.

Pooja adds, "But I also brought toys for your daughter." Manoj replies, "Then let's go home; give them to me yourself."

It seems Pooja is trying to make an excuse, as if she doesn't want to go inside the house. Manoj doesn't press the issue too much but insists, "Pooja, it's fine to give me the books, but you should hand over the toys yourself."

Pooja responds, "You're right, but it won't look good if I give you the books but don't give the toys I brought for the child. I promised last time we met, and I'm not the kind of person who forgets promises to move ahead in life. So, please take these toys and give them to the child on my behalf; it will make me very happy."After a while, when Pooja leaves, Manoj arrives home, his daughter and Gudiya are waiting for him.

As soon as Gudiya sees him, she asks, "What happened? You're very late today."

Manoj replies, "Yes, Pooja came to see how the children were practicing during the training session. It took a while to show her everything."

Gudiya notices the bundle of books in Manoj's hands and asks, "What are these?"

Manoj replies, "Oh, it's nothing. Pooja knows I like to read, so she brought me some books. And look, she also brought toys for you."

Gudiya asks, "Did she not come home with you?"

Manoj replies, "No, she had to go somewhere else, and she left from the ground."

Gudiya says, "Oh..."

Manoj continues, "The children were very happy to see her. If the district collector comes to encourage the children, it's a big deal. Many children get inspired by that."

Gudiya replies, "That's true; children will be inspired by the collector. What inspiration can they get from a housewife like me?" Hearing Gudiya's words, Manoj is taken aback; he didn't expect her to say something like that.

Manoj tries to handle the situation, saying, "No, that's not true. Everyone has their importance and place." Gudiya lightly laughs and replies, "Such words are very soothing for deceiving oneself."

Instead of dragging the conversation, Manoj thinks it's better to end it there and says, "You're unnecessarily comparing yourself, and why such things suddenly? Is there something on your mind?"

Gudiya replies, "What could it be? There's nothing; I was just saying that."

After this, Gudiya reluctantly walks towards the kitchen. Manoj watches her for a moment and then starts feeding the child lying on the bed, coaxing her.

A woman has this inner strength that helps her sense potential dangers that could come between her and her loved ones. That day, this inner strength was making Gudiya restless.

# Chapter 26

Two days later, Manoj received a call from Pritam Singh's agency, informing him that the agency had decided to stop sponsoring Manoj's academy. Manoj couldn't understand this sudden decision and said he would talk to Pritam Singh.

When he spoke to Pritam Singh, Manoj asked, "What is this, Pritam Ji? You can't just stop sponsoring the academy suddenly. The children have been practicing for so long; their future is at stake."

Pritam Singh replied, "But we cannot put our company's future at risk for the children's future. The livelihoods of people here could be at stake; will you run their homes?"

"Finally, what happened, Pritam Ji, that you are saying this?" Manoj inquired.

Pritam Singh said, "We do business, and business doesn't run on emotions, Manoj Ji. We have been sponsoring your academy for the past year, but we haven't found any child from your academy who can promote our branding on a national level. Those two girls of yours, Lakhaniya and Baby, haven't made any impact either. They didn't even make it to the runner-up in the national games; they were behind in the first or second place. After such poor performance, how can you expect us to continue investing money in you?"

Manoj replied, "So, do you think, Pritam Singh Ji, that you can get results in just a couple of attempts? It takes time; patience is necessary to reach desired results. If you expect results overnight, you are setting yourself up for disappointment. Achieving big goals requires effort."

Pritam Singh responded, "We are business people, Manoj Ji. We don't invest in shares that show no potential for profit. Instead, we withdraw money from shares that are losing and invest it where there's gain. Your two girls have lost in the national games, which clearly indicates they will never play at the national level again. Moreover, there hasn't been any response from your academy in the last few months that suggests your children will achieve outstanding results to reach the national level. We are also in contact with several other academies whose children are regularly being selected."

"We came to help you, but for our benefit. Our company's idea was to contract players as they rise so that when they win national competitions, the branding benefits our company at very low rates. Because after winning at the national level, a player gains a national image, and contracting them becomes quite expensive. But in your case, you have not lived up to our expectations."

Manoj responded, "Pritam Ji, sports should be taken in the spirit of sportsmanship. If you take it with a business mindset, good players will never be developed."

Pritam Singh replied, "So how will good players be developed, Manoj Ji? We have been providing you all the facilities for the past year. But can you now guarantee that in the next national games, the players from your academy will make it?"

Manoj thought for a moment and said, "Yes, why wouldn't they make it? I have full faith in them."

Pritam Singh replied, "In business, there is no faith, Manoj Ji; there are contracts. If you have faith, then give us a written contract, and we will continue your sponsorship, but on our terms. If it doesn't happen, you will return all the money our company spends on you during this period, and you will need to provide some guarantees."

Manoj fell silent. Now he had nothing more to say.

Pritam Singh said, "See, Manoj Ji, your faith in this contract has already shaken; what can I say now? You can understand very well what will happen next."

Manoj said, "Pritam Ji, dreams are achieved through the strength of the heart, not through calculations. I haven't done so much calculation."

Pritam started laughing, "One must think, Manoj Ji. A wise person is one who helps others rise without falling himself."

Manoj was staring intently at Pritam Singh's business acumen, thinking that this man was only concerned about profits. Noticing Manoj's silence, Pritam Singh said, "Now you know what we should do. It's better to move forward with those sports academies whose players have already been selected this time. This is also the rule of business and understanding. In this situation, investing further in Manoj and his academy would not be beneficial; rather, they would look for some other endorsement route."

Manoj had no words left to say. He quietly listened to Pritam Singh's words.

That evening, during the children's practice at his academy, Manoj came as usual but was worried, and Chandan sensed this concern. After practice, Chandan asked Manoj, "What's wrong? Why are you so troubled?"

Manoj explained everything to Chandan. Essentially, Manoj expressed that he had recently selected some new girls and it was not possible to withdraw from this commitment because they had planned to train these new girls based on sponsorship. Many of these girls came from family backgrounds where they could barely earn two meals a day. Manoj told Chandan, "We have already selected other children, and we will have to determine our future path based on these children. If we retreat now, we will also be seen as frauds in the eyes of the world."

Chandan questioned, "So, what should we do now?" There wasn't enough money to run the academy solely on its own. Manoj added that they shouldn't discuss financial help or fees with the children's families because they had announced during selection that they would cover all expenses for the training of any child they selected.

In this situation, expecting any kind of financial assistance from the families of those children was wrong. And if any kind of fee were to be demanded, it would send the message that Manoj was doing this free training stunt just to earn money for the sports academy, which would make him look like a fraud. Manoj didn't want to move forward with this stigma.

Finding another sponsor quickly seemed unlikely. The bigger issue was that if a new sponsor was found, questions would inevitably arise about why the previous sponsor had pulled out. How would the rent for the leased ground be paid? Who would cover the food and dietary needs of the children during training, which Manoj had been managing? Then there were expenses for essentials like shoes and shorts, along with travel costs for children participating in championships. Pritam Singh's agency had been covering all these expenses for the past year, but now Manoj had to manage everything on his own.

Moreover, there was a district-level championship at the end of this year, and it was crucial to train new children so that at least some could be selected for the state level. If training was stopped, it would become difficult to make it to the district level, and if the results came out as zero again, everything would be over.

On the other hand, the loss of Lakhaniya and Baby in the National Games sent a very negative message, and people felt that the bubble of Lakhaniya and Baby's victory had burst. Manoj didn't want to unnecessarily pressure Lakhaniya and Baby, as he was aware of their mental state. He wanted to prepare both girls mentally just like before.

That night, Manoj pondered for a long time and then decided that he was willing to put his ancestral home as a guarantee in front of

Pritam's company. He was confident that this time, at least one child from their academy would surely be selected in the upcoming National Games.

Chandan was taken aback by his thoughts. He warned Manoj, "What are you saying? Are you going to put your house as collateral, and what if no child gets selected? Will you end up on the streets with your wife and children? Think practically, brother." Chandan completely disagreed with Manoj's plan. In his view, it was a suicidal idea. He pointed out that Manoj had just seen the condition of Lakhaniya and Baby. If something similar happened again, Manoj would be left with nothing.

Chandan continued, "It's good to do something for others, but you can't destroy yourself to build castles for them."

Manoj interrupted him, "Why do you think I am doing this for others? This is the fire within me, brother. If I don't do this, the question is, what will I do? This inner fire will consume me. Suppose I turn out to be wrong; then it will still be the same. It's better to be consumed while trying than to be consumed without doing anything. At least there is a possibility that everything will be okay."

Chandan replied, "But you are not alone now; you have a family. There are responsibilities."

Manoj responded, "I know that is why this time I will give it my all to ensure that there is no chance of failure.

Chandan- But I don't know why I feel like you are getting emotional, just thinking sentimentally."

Manoj continued, "I'm not emotional, Chandan, but I don't want to think so much about losing that it starts to feel like winning is impossible. I have some easier paths as well; if I can't do anything, I will follow those paths."

Chandan asked, "And what are those paths?"

Manoj replied, "If I can't do anything, Chandan, I will go to Delhi and start teaching. I have many old friends in good places; they will help me in some way."

Chandan retorted, "So you are going to leave certainty and head towards an uncertain goal? Planning to gamble your settled home for a chance of wandering around?" He questioned, "What guarantee do you have that those friends will come through for you?"

Manoj replied, "Chandan, don't weaken my morale. Right now, I don't want to think about who will help me if my plan fails and how. I just want to focus on how to win the challenge I'm choosing for myself. There are seven billion people in this world, and more than half of them can manage two meals a day. I don't see myself as so weak that I can't manage those two meals for myself or my family. My real challenge is my dream; that's the real fight, the real struggle. I've lost my dream once in life, and I don't want to lose again. I'm ready to take any risk for that."

Chandan realized that Manoj was not going to agree with him. He said, "Go home and think everything over. Meet me tomorrow. Talk to Gudiya about this issue too. Then let me know."

After speaking with Chandan, when Manoj returned home, he decided to tell Gudiya that he was considering putting their house as collateral for Pritam Singh's company, but Gudiya was already upset before meeting Manoj and Pooja, so he felt this was not the right time. He also anticipated that Gudiya would never agree to this.

The next morning, Manoj went to Gudiya and said he needed to discuss something important. Gudiya froze for a moment, and Manoj informed her that Pritam Singh's company had refused to provide funding for the academy, and now they had no money to run it. Hearing this, Gudiya became anxious.

Gudiya asked, "What will happen now?"

Manoj replied, "Something will happen. A new problem has arisen, and we must face it bravely."

Gudiya said, "That's true, but how will we do it? We have to do something to avoid the problem."

Upon hearing this, Manoj explained everything that had happened with Pritam Singh in detail.

Manoj said, "Now we have only one option: we must provide some guarantee to Pritam's company so that our sponsorship does not end."

Gudiya asked, "But what do we have to offer as a guarantee? Is there anyone else who can help?"

Manoj replied, "I've decided that we will put our home as collateral."

Hearing this, Gudiya became utterly upset.

"Have you lost your mind? What are you saying?" Gudiya continued, "You invested your time, effort, and money in Lakhaniya and Baby, but in the end, they left you, right? The same outcome will happen again. Why should I risk our child's future for the future of others' children? I know we don't have much right now, but what we have is enough to live well."

Gudiya tells Manoj that this last piece of land is her child's future, and she doesn't want to gamble that future on any uncertain possibility that may or may not prove right.

Manoj explains to Gudiya that this is the last chance; nothing will be proven wrong. Gudiya was not in a position to take any risks at the cost of her child. Manoj was also adamant that he didn't want to be proven false in front of the world; he had come too far, and facing this challenge was the best way forward. He felt that risks must be taken if they were to move toward their dreams. Manoj said he didn't want to remain a defeated father in front of his child. When my child grows up,

I don't want him to say that my father prepared for the IAS but failed, ran a shop but failed, and ran an academy but also failed, putting at risk the future of those children connected to him. I don't want my child to see me like this.

Gudiya responded, "Such emotional talks won't prove you right. Until now, I have stood by your every decision, right or wrong, fulfilling my duties as a wife. Even when you left me during the childbirth, I managed to convince myself, thinking there must have been some compulsions on your part. But now I feel I was wrong. You have become selfish, thinking only of yourself; neither do I matter to you, nor the child, nor our family. The only thing that matters to you is your stubbornness. Such stubbornness that leads to nothing but trouble."

Manoj was not willing to accept that he was selfish and only thinking about himself, but he was also unable to reassure Gudiya with his words. For a whole week, there was tension between Manoj and Gudiya regarding this matter. Manoj hoped that Gudiya would agree. The academy ran by Manoj was on rented land, and the rent was due soon; thus, he had to decide what to do. One day, Manoj went to meet Pritam Singh with Chandan and spoke about his village house as collateral.

Pritam Singh refused his proposal and said that Manoj should be grateful to the company that they were not charging him any rent or fees for this equipment. Otherwise, just think, you would have become indebted to us too.

Manoj replied, "If you care so much about professional ethics, then why are you putting the future of my academy's children at stake? Uphold your ethics; on one hand, you are demanding a guarantee that the next time, the children will be selected nationally. On the other hand, you are playing such a game."

Pritam Singh said, "There's no need to discuss all this nonsense now, and I don't have time to waste with you all day. It would be better if you leave here now." Until now, Chandan had been listening to everything, but seeing Pritam Singh talk so rudely made Chandan speak up, "Is this how you talk? Are you out of your mind?"

Pritam Singh replied, "I have asked you to leave respectfully; otherwise, I will call the security guard right now." Pritam rang the bell to call the security guard.

Manoj took Chandan's hand and began to leave. Once outside, Manoj sat outside Pritam Singh's company for a long time. His mind was filled with anger, and he felt like giving Pritam Singh a good thrashing. In fact, often a person does not feel angry when they are being mistreated; they feel anger later when they think about that mistreatment. They think about it repeatedly, their self-esteem is shattered, and they feel helpless. True anger arises then. The same was happening with Manoj. Seeing Manoj's condition, Chandan said, "You stay here; I will go out to get some food and see if we can find a ride to the station." Saying this, Chandan went outside.

Manoj's mind was racing with thoughts. He felt that Pritam Singh had betrayed him and had also insulted him greatly. While he was lost in these thoughts, Pritam Singh came outside; his car had arrived. Upon seeing Manoj, he said, "Oh, you didn't leave yet? It seems you'll leave only after getting kicked out."

That was the last straw; Manoj lost his mind and slapped Pritam Singh hard. His staff and guards intervened to protect Pritam Singh from the onslaught of kicks and punches, and they restrained Manoj. Manoj had lost control. Anyone who came in front of him was targeted. Somehow, Manoj was subdued. Pritam Singh had called the police. When Chandan returned, he saw that a fight had broken out and the police were taking Manoj away. Chandan hid and watched the whole scene; he was afraid that if he stepped in, Pritam Singh's people might frame him with false charges and send him to jail.

That evening, Manoj was sitting at the police station when Chandan somehow arrived with two people from his contacts in that city and spoke to the police about Manoj. The police told them that he had been brought in for a fight. They would need to arrange bail for his release.

The station chief said that Pritam Singh had made serious allegations, serious charges would be filed in the FIR, and Manoj would face a long jail sentence. Chandan's heart sank at this news. He pleaded with the station chief for help, but the chief said if they could arrange some money, they would apply lighter charges. It would make it easier to get bail. At that time, Chandan did not have any money, and this new complication arose. Manoj was the only person in his acquaintance who could handle such matters, and now he was in trouble himself.

Chandan somehow reached Manoj in the police lockup and asked if he could get help from Collector Pooja. Manoj told Chandan not to ask for help from her. It is human nature not to want to show their wounds to lost love; it would only make their helplessness feel worse. Manoj felt that he had distanced himself from Pooja thinking he didn't want to burden her; how could he become a burden to her now? At least by doing this, Manoj wanted to maintain his self-worth; otherwise, losing both love and self-respect would be extremely painful.

Chandan did not understand why Manoj was saying this. But there was no time for Chandan to question Manoj about it. Instead, Manoj gave Chandan the number of his friend Vivek, who was currently the Joint Commissioner in the Income Tax Department in Kolkata. Manoj told Chandan that Vivek was his room partner in Delhi. He asked Chandan to call him and explain the situation; he might help. When Chandan called Vivek and explained everything, Vivek contacted some IPS officers and requested them to help Manoj.

Upon Vivek's request, when the police station where Manoj was detained received the call, the station chief told Vivek that the FIR had already been registered. The complainants were also making calls from important places, and they had to take immediate action. If your call had come a little earlier, I might have been in a position to help. Now it would have to go through the court for bail.

As soon as the call ended, the station chief told the clerk to quickly write the FIR as calls were coming in for intervention. If the FIR was not written, it would create problems.

In fact, Pritam Singh had instructed the police to apply extortion charges against Manoj in a vengeful spirit for the beating and had even paid a service fee for it. After accepting the service fee, the station chief could not back out of Pritam Singh's demands; otherwise, he would face embarrassment. Therefore, he falsely informed his higher-ups that the FIR had been written, and now it would have to be resolved through the court.

After a while, when Chandan returned to meet Manoj at the police station, the station chief chased Chandan away, saying, "Go and get bail from the court now." Manoj had already told Chandan to call Lakhaniya and Baby in the village and inform them to continue training the children who come to the academy daily. Chandan did just that.

When problems arise, they do not come from just one direction but from all sides, entangling everything completely. The day this incident happened was a Sunday holiday, and after that, there were two days of public holidays due to the festival, so the court was closed. In such a situation, getting bail for Manoj was now difficult.

Another issue was that Chandan didn't have money for a lawyer or bail bonds, but as a true friend, he wanted to help Manoj out of this problem and take him back to the village. He was afraid that if he returned alone, he wouldn't know what to tell Gudiya.

There is a reason why it is said that a calm mind is essential to tackle problems; this incident proved that when a person is in trouble, they should distance themselves from anything that could worsen their situation. However, when destruction is imminent, the mind works against one's interests; during bad times, a person can be insulted even when they show respect, and when good times begin, people will overlook bad behavior as if it were a blessing.

Manoj was going through a tough time. He even told Chandan not to worry too much; he would either manage as best as he could or return to the village. He said he would come back when he got time.

Chandan was at a loss; he had never dealt with the police or courts in his life. So, he did what he thought was best. He called someone in the village and borrowed thirty thousand rupees, then contacted a good lawyer in the city and explained the whole situation. Solutions often lie within problems, and the fortunate part was that the lawyer was the younger brother of a high court judge and was very reasonable. He assured Chandan that there was a good chance of getting bail on the first date. That's exactly what happened, and after a full six days, Manoj appeared in court and was granted bail.

# Chapter 27

Life is a drama filled with suspense, and just when you think the story is over, it takes an unexpected turn. Manoj returned to the village but found him trapped in a new emotional predicament despite escaping previous troubles. Meanwhile, Gudiya, upset with the situation at home, had gone back to her maternal home.

The villagers were unaware of the police station and court incidents that had taken place in the city. Gudiya was resentful that Manoj decided to use their house as collateral despite her objections. Moreover, he left for the city without informing her and had Chandan call her upon arrival instead of speaking to her directly. These incidents deeply hurt Gudiya, as a wife tends to believe she holds a unique and irreplaceable place in her husband's life. Manoj's actions seemed to indicate a lack of trust and disregard for her feelings, which weighed heavily on her mind. Unable to bear it, she packed her belongings and left with their child for her maternal home. There, she simply told her family that Manoj had gone to the city for work and she had come to visit.

Gudiya firmly believed that serious issues in a marriage should be resolved privately between husband and wife, without involving others. However, this time the emotional distance between her and Manoj had grown so vast that she felt the need for some time apart. Often, time has a way of naturally healing problems.

Manoj was deeply shaken by Gudiya's departure. When communication breaks down, dialogue becomes essential for mending relationships. However, a lack of trust only widens the gap further. Their relationship suffered under these circumstances, and neither wanted to take the first step toward reconciliation.

Gudiya's absence left Manoj emotionally devastated. He was unsure of what to do next. From his failure in the UPSC exams, Manoj had learned that prolonged struggles often lead to compromise rather than empowerment. This wasn't limited to specific events but applied to every aspect of an ordinary person's life. Extended struggles require immense mental strength, something not everyone possesses, nor is it always possible. As a result, people often resign to circumstances, accepting them conditionally. While this can bring stability in some cases, in others, it's akin to turning a blind eye to injustices, sometimes at the cost of one's self-respect.

In the evening, Lakhaniya and Baby visited Manoj and informed him that the landlord had come to collect rent, and representatives from Pritam Singh's company had taken away all the equipment. They also handed over a notice demanding compensation for damages, amounting to fifty thousand. Manoj explained to Lakhaniya and Baby everything that had transpired in the city. Hearing this, they, too, grew concerned.

Manoj advised them to stay focused on their game, emphasizing that if they didn't give their best in the upcoming state and national championships, all their efforts so far would go to waste. He stressed that their preparation was more important than even keeping the sports academy running.

Understanding the gravity of the situation, Lakhaniya and Baby promised Manoj that they would put in their best efforts and avoid all distractions. Manoj assured them that he would find a solution and arrange the required money in the next few days to prevent the academy from shutting down. He instructed them to continue their practice sessions with the other girls in the meantime. Once the financial issues would be resolved, he would devise a strategy for their training to ensure they could win the upcoming championships.

Both girls reassured Manoj of their dedication, and Manoj felt confident in their determination. Meanwhile, Chandan was also dealing with financial pressures, as people had started approaching him to recover the money he had borrowed to secure Manoj's release from police custody.One evening, Chandan came to Manoj's house to discuss the matter. By then, it had been two days since Manoj had returned from the city. Finding Manoj sitting quietly on the rooftop, Chandan went straight up to him.

Chandan: "What's going on, brother? Sitting up here?"

Manoj didn't respond. Sensing the gravity of the situation, Chandan understood that things were serious.

Chandan: "Did you talk to Gudiya? Has she said anything about when she'll return from her maternal home?"

Manoj finally broke his silence: "No, I haven't spoken to her."

Chandan: "Why not?"

Manoj: "I didn't think it was necessary."

Chandan couldn't understand. "What do you mean by 'not necessary'? If you avoid addressing the issue like this, it'll only get worse. Call her or talk to her. Explain what happened in the city—she'll understand."

Manoj: "I don't want to explain anything to her right now. How can I even face her when I'm in the wrong? She told me not to use the house as collateral, but I didn't listen. And what happened? I made a mistake. What right do I have to show my face to her?"

Chandan: "Brother, she's your wife. If you don't share your feelings with her, who else will you share? Maybe I've read fewer books than you, but let me offer you a piece of advice—don't take it the wrong way."

Manoj looked up at Chandan.

Chandan: "Look, women care deeply, which is why they often give advice, even when it's not asked for. They expect the same care and understanding from men. They want their words to be heard and supported because they offer that same care to the men in their lives. "But men, on the other hand, prioritize trust above all. A man will love a woman more if she proves that she trusts him, even if she doesn't always agree with him or spend much time with him. If a man feels that the woman will stand by him no matter what, he values her deeply.

However, when a woman's care turns into constant unsolicited advice, it can weaken that sense of trust, and the man starts to drift away from her care. Similarly, if a woman doesn't feel her words are valued or supported by her partner, she begins to think he doesn't care for her. This imbalance leads to bigger conflicts, just like the one you and Gudiya are facing." Manoj listened intently and replied: "I didn't expect you to explain such a big truth in such simple words. Is this experience speaking?"

Chandan laughed. "Call it experience if you like."

Manoj continued: "The problem lies in how differently we approach love. We spend our whole lives studying math, science, physics, chemistry, profit, loss, and management, but never do we study love. We treat it as unimportant, something that doesn't deserve even one lesson, yet ironically, it's the one thing we expect to receive from everyone without understanding it. We live formulaic, textbook lives and expect love to fit into the same formulas."

Manoj added: "Luck plays such a big role in life. I had a friend in Delhi, Pintu, who used to say life is like a wave—lambda between life and death. You think you're scripting it with your courage and hard work, but eventually, you realize it's taking you where fate wants you to go. We have so little to control over our circumstances.

"Half my life has passed, and what have I done? As a child, I saw my father work tirelessly and dreamed of becoming his strength. When I grew up, I became a burden. He spent all his money on my education, took on debts, and passed away under that burden. I couldn't achieve anything before he died. I loved Puja but couldn't be with her. I wanted to succeed in sports, but financial hardships keep pulling me back. Now my wife and child have left me. Everything is falling apart, Chandan. Life defeats me at every step... every single step."

Manoj became deeply emotional as he spoke. Chandan placed Manoj's head on his shoulder and consoled him, assuring him that things would get better. For the first time, Chandan learned about Manoj's past with Puja, but he refrained from probing further, knowing Manoj was already burdened by his circumstances.

A few days passed. Manoj developed a high fever and felt dizzy constantly. Despite being aware of his health, he neglected it, thinking it was just seasonal fever, and relied on paracetamol. However, his condition worsened. Feeling helpless, Manoj decided to visit a doctor but first went to Chandan's house for company. Unfortunately, Chandan was out of town on urgent work, so Manoj resolved to go alone.

On that day, due to a Chief Minister's event in a nearby town, all public transport was halted for security reasons. Manoj had no choice but to walk four kilometers to the doctor's clinic under the scorching sun. Weak and exhausted, he barely managed to walk a kilometer, dizziness overwhelmed him, and he collapsed by the roadside. Passersby gathered around, and someone informed the police.

Coincidentally, among the officers was the assistant sub-inspector(ASI) who had previously escorted Puja to Manoj's house months ago. Recognizing Manoj as a friend of the Collector, the ASI decided to convey  this information to Puja.

When Puja received the news, she instructed her staff to bring Manoj to the Collector's residence and arrange for a doctor. "I'll join as soon as the Chief Minister's program concludes," she said.

Manoj remained in a state of half-consciousness throughout the night as his treatment continued. By morning, his condition improved, and he fully regained his senses. Pooja was sitting beside him. She asked, "How are you feeling now?"

Manoj replied, "Much better than before. It was a fever—I've had it dozens of times before, but this time it was different. My hands and legs cramped, and the fever wouldn't go down. That's why I was heading to see a doctor, but I collapsed on the way."

Pooja said, "You've got dengue. Your platelet count is very low; you're still in danger. You'll receive proper treatment here. By the way, where are your wife and child? Last night, you told my staff that no one was at home."

Manoj responded, "She's at her parents' place with our daughter. I didn't want to stress them out."Pooja suggested, "Then stay here and get treated. Once you're better, you can go home." Pooja secretly wished to spend some time with Manoj.

Manoj hesitated, "Staying with you—"Pooja interrupted, "Oh, this Collector's residence is just a name; it's more like a government office. Everyone goes about their work here. My staff lives here, too. I'll also be staying here."

Manoj understood that Pooja was reassuring him that there was nothing improper for anyone to question. Manoj was very weak and felt dizzy even while trying to stand. Pooja called the doctor. Upon seeing the reports, the doctor stated that it would take at least ten days for him to recover and that platelets would need to be transfused. Pooja asked the doctor and her staff to arrange everything, and they promptly got to work.

Pooja then left Manoj's room to focus on her official tasks but checked on him periodically throughout the day. After dinner, Pooja would return to Manoj's room and rest on a chair beside him, leaving the doors and windows open so that the helpers and staff wouldn't misunderstand.

Late at night, when Manoj would wake up, he'd often see Pooja sitting in the chair—sometimes reading files, sometimes closing her eyes, and sometimes staring at him intently. By the third day, Manoj's condition had significantly improved. One night, when he woke up, he saw Pooja looking at him. His eyes moved to the wall clock—it was quarter to three.

Manoj said, "Go to sleep, Pooja. You've been staying here all night for three days. You'll fall sick this way."

Pooja replied, "No, let me stay here. It gives me peace. Don't you want me to find some moments of tranquility in life?"

Manoj said, "You work all day, and if you stay awake all night, how will you recover from fatigue?"

Pooja answered, "When your soul is tired, the body doesn't tire easily. If my presence here bothers you, I'll leave."

Manoj responded, "Oh no, why would it bother me? I was just worried seeing you awake."

Pooja said, "Then let me stay here with you. Don't I have at least this much right to sit in front of you and watch over you?"

Manoj gazed at her silently.Pooja continued, "Fate separated us, and now that we finally have this moment, do you want to take it away as well?"

Manoj noticed the same yearning in Pooja's eyes.

He asked, "So, what do you want? For me to remain sick here so you can keep looking at me like this?"

Pooja chuckled, "Your enemies should fall sick! I can't even see you like this while you're here. And once you recover and leave, will I ever get such a chance to sit beside you again?"

Manoj fell silent. He didn't know what to say to Pooja's words. After a few moments of quiet, Pooja spoke again.

"When someone you've been separated from for years suddenly reappears, it's hard to know what to say. Should you talk about the past? Should you tell them how much effort went into finding them — how many evenings and nights were spent? Should you tell them how their little quirks were treasured in your memories, cherished like a prayer? Would they even believe you? Even if they did, what's the use? Life has already moved on. Those moments belong to a past that's long gone.

But if you don't say anything, then why did you try so hard to find them? Why did your heart keep searching for them? That question will always sting." She paused, then continued, "People are attached to their good memories. They keep returning to them. Sensitive people do this even more. Sometimes, for the sake of the people you care about, it's important to let them live their lives happily, without interfering in their world."

Manoj listened intently and, after she finished, said, "Sometimes, maintaining a respectful distance keeps both relationships and memories beautiful forever."

The conversation between Pooja and Manoj flowed seamlessly.

Manoj asked, "Pooja, where is your husband? A few years ago, Vivek mentioned that you had married an IAS officer."

Pooja sighed deeply, "Yes, I married Ashish."

Manoj replied, "Yes, that's the name he mentioned. I heard he comes from a very influential family."

Pooja nodded, "Yes, Ashish's father was a DGP, his mother an IAS officer. His sister is a CEO of a company, and her husband is a prominent name in real estate. It's a very strong family."

Manoj asked, "Then you—?"

Pooja interrupted, "Then what? We live separately. Just a few months after the marriage, I realized that we were two people from completely different worlds. Our thoughts were poles apart. The things Ashish enjoyed suffocated me. We were fundamentally incompatible. When ambition turns into a pursuit of power, loneliness takes over."

Ashish seeks power, and I long for love. In such a situation, neither of us could give the other what they needed. Even the most dishonest person desires honesty for themselves, but that's not how it works. Nature returns to you what you give to it. Thus, this outcome in my relationship with Ashish was inevitable.

Now the divorce case is in process, and soon it will be granted. I'll finally be free of this entanglement."

Manoj replied, "Oh, that's unfortunate. But why marry in the first place if you didn't realize this earlier?"

Hearing this, Pooja glared at Manoj sharply.

Pooja said, "You should be the one standing in the dock for that question. If you hadn't left me like a coward, I would have been very happy today. All I ever wanted was to be with you. I had even cleared my IAS selection. But you abandoned me, and for that, I will never forgive you."

As she spoke, Pooja's voice cracked, and her throat tightened with emotion. She tried hard to hold back, but the pain buried inside her for years was desperate to break free. With a trembling voice, she said, "Today, I am all alone. After you, I couldn't accept anyone else. Whenever I met someone, I would see your image in them and couldn't connect with them. You may have left me, but I could never distance myself from you."

Manoj felt a deep sense of regret upon hearing this.

Before he could say anything, one of Pooja's staff members arrived with tea.

"Ma'am, tea," the staff member said. Pooja composed herself, swiftly drying the streaks of tears on her face with her inner strength. A clerk accompanied the staff member, holding some files. He handed them to Pooja and said, "Ma'am, these files need to be dispatched today."

Pooja took the files and began reading them. Manoj silently observed her, marvelling at how quickly she masked her emotions. He felt a surge of guilt, realizing how such a cheerful person had become so adept at suppressing her feelings.

After signing the files, Pooja handed them back to the staff, who left the room.

Manoj said, "Pooja, I went back to meet you. But you were away for field training. I met Vivek there, and he told me that Ashish had proposed to you. I was going through such a rough time that I couldn't muster the courage to meet you. I even boarded a train to Dehradun but got off halfway. I was plagued by fears back then. And when a person is scared, they can't make the right decisions. That's exactly what happened to me."

Pooja responded, "You know, Manoj, in true love, a failed person either spends the rest of their life in penance or vengeance... there's no other way out. You've been trapped in the same cycle. Your biggest flaw was that after a negative outcome, you lost faith in yourself. And when you couldn't trust yourself, how could you trust people like me, who wanted to connect with you?"

Saying this, Pooja left for her bedroom. Meanwhile, Manoj lay on the bed, consumed by remorse, reflecting on the wrong decision he had made.

Even the smallest decisions in life have long-lasting impacts, shaping its course. His decision to separate from Pooja was not just a mistake—it was a catastrophic one.

# Chapter 28

The next day, Chandan arrived at the Collector's residence while searching for Manoj. Chandan told Manoj that he should go home as soon as he got better. Chandan would go and persuade Gudiya to come back home. Manoj agreed with Chandan's suggestion. Manoj then asked if Lakhaniya and Baby were training or not. After meeting both of them, Chandan replied that he had just returned from the city and had come here. After leaving here, he would see what the training environment was like.

But Chandan's question was how long would all this go on? Manoj couldn't even decide how he would deal with all these troubles together. Manoj said, "When a problem arises, Chandan, it comes from all sides and torments a person. The academy's landowner will again demand rent.

They don't have a penny left now. It seems we will have to close the academy this time. The Commonwealth Games are next year, and if we have to send Lakhaniya and Baby there, they should start preparing at war level. Besides, after being dropped from the national team, the way both of them have lost their confidence, they will have to exert themselves to regain their morale."

Chandan: They will have to put in effort, but how will they do it? There is no academy, you are unwell. Money was also spent on fighting with Pritam Singh, and there are separate debts, and there is also a court appearance coming up next week. Bhabi has left, and you are preparing to sell your father's house. Do you have anything left? Think about yourself, Manoj; my brother, the troubles are escalating. Manoj: So besides selling the house, is there any option left? The girls we selected, whose parents trusted us and left their children with us. Should we send them back so they can collect money in the name of fees? We were selecting them under the name of free training, right? We urgently need a large sum of money. How will it come, or should we just give up?

Chandan: It's better to raise our hands than to be ruined.

Manoj: It's not that easy. Once trust is broken, people won't reconnect. Secondly, opportunities don't come around often. We were very close to success; if Pritam hadn't deceived us, the circumstances were in our favor.

As Chandan and Manoj continued their conversation, Pooja entered the room. Both fell silent, not wanting to speak in front of her, but they were unaware that Pooja had overheard their conversation while walking outside, and she had come in after listening to them.

Pooja: You're in such trouble, Manoj, and you didn't even tell me.

Chandan was surprised to see Pooja speaking so warmly with Manoj, but he didn't let his emotions show on his face. At that moment, Pooja sat down and started to understand all the problems, discussing solutions with Manoj. She had already spoken to a lawyer in the city regarding the Pritam Singh case and discussed all aspects of resolving the issue as soon as possible. Additionally, she asked Manoj if he would be willing to join the academy if she made arrangements for land and a sports ground for training.

Pooja knew this was a big task, and starting any academy on government resources could take a lot of time. Therefore, she offered to give fifty thousand rupees from her salary as rent for the sports academy so that the children's training wouldn't be disrupted until an alternative arrangement was made. Manoj and Chandan were astonished at how Pooja managed to control the troubles that had brought them to the brink of ruin in an instant. Chandan was speechless witnessing the bond between Manoj and Pooja.

Manoj tried to convince Pooja not to give her hard-earned fifty thousand rupees. He said he would arrange for it, but Pooja scolded him.

Pooja: What will you arrange, Manoj? Will you mortgage your house? What wrong did Gudiya do to leave you after fighting? After all, every mother will think first about her child's future. Let me tell you, Manoj, you only think about yourself, and that's why you and I are at two different ends. Even today, you're making the same mistake. You cannot stake Gudiya and the child's secure future for your plans and decisions.

Manoj felt embarrassed and didn't want to respond to Pooja's remarks. He could only say that as soon as he managed to arrange the money, he would return it to her.

Pooja laughed in frustration.

Pooja: Manoj, are you seriously this foolish or cunning? I can't understand you. Did I ask you for money that you would return it? If there was ever any emotion between us during this phase of life and you respected it, you wouldn't say such foolish things. If you had married me instead of Gudiya, would you have been burdened by this kind of gratitude for my money? No, you wouldn't have. But perhaps you don't respect me anymore, which is why you walk around with such a heavy heart. You had so many problems, and despite living in the same district, you didn't find it appropriate to tell me anything.

Manoj just kept looking at Pooja, while Chandan watched both of them.

The next day, Pooja was in front of the Collector's office, where the district's sports officer, Vijay Kumar, was standing. Manoj was also sitting there. Pooja introduced Manoj to Vijay and asked about the availability of funds for sports development in the district. It turned out that the government had allocated some money for the fund, which had not been spent and would be returned to the government by the end of the financial year.

When Pooja asked why the money hadn't been spent, Vijay began to look away. The truth was, Vijay Kumar was a lazy man, and during his four-year posting in this district, he hadn't done anything except draw his salary. He hadn't started any planned activities, funded any sports competitions, or worked on any special strategy to train athletes. He would occasionally show up at annual sports competitions in various schools and colleges, and if a letter came from the department, he would write a report to keep the file showing sports development.

Pooja was very angry seeing the state of sports in her district. She first asked Vijay Kumar to provide a written explanation for why disciplinary action shouldn't be taken against him for his negligent behavior regarding sports development in the district. Vijay assured her that he would provide a written explanation and defended himself by stating that there was no seriousness regarding sports development in the district. If any block, panchayat, or institution worked on something, people only showed enthusiasm for the misuse of government funds. Thus, Vijay was clear that people didn't want the development of sports but only their own.

Pooja shouted, "It is your job to stop all this, Vijay, which you are not doing while standing here telling stories. If you don't want strict action against you, then show some improvement. This will not only benefit the youth of this district but also you."

Vijay responded, "Yes, Sir." Manoj was watching everything. After this, Pooja said, "This is Manoj; he trains girls in athletics, and the girls trained by him are getting selected at the state level. Do you know him?"

Vijay replied that he didn't recognize him but perhaps had met him before. Manoj immediately reminded Vijay that they had met at several sports competitions, but Mr. Vijay Gupta quickly contradicted him, saying, "Yes, we have met, but have you ever proposed to organize any sports? If you had, we would certainly have made some plans." In fact, Vijay was focused only on claiming he was fully committed to sports development, but despite that, he wasn't getting any support from the public or the athletes, which hindered the development of sports in the district.

Pooja told Vijay that if there was government land in Manoj's panchayat, they needed to plan for developing a sports ground there. She told him to devise a strategy for it and come back with a complete plan. "This is your last chance to prove your worth; otherwise, a careless and indifferent person like you shouldn't remain in government service. As soon as Manoj leaves my chamber, you can meet him to get all the details."

Upon hearing this, Vijay left Pooja's chamber.

Now Manoj was sitting in front of Pooja in the chamber. Manoj said that if a place for sports was identified, it would be a significant accomplishment for that area. Pooja agreed, saying that if it happened, the sports ground would be open for everyone, and anyone could come and work for sports there.

Manoj suggested to Pooja that an arrangement could be made so that only members could use the sports ground. This way, serious athletes would come to that ground, and it would remain safe from the intrusion of rowdy or troublesome people. If the sports ground was left open like this, it would quickly become a den of mischief, and unwanted people would take it over. Consequently, serious players or girls wouldn't be able to practice or play there.

Pooja agreed with this suggestion and assured Manoj that this would be taken into account. After that, Manoj, Pooja, and Vijay Kumar worked at a war footing on developing the strategy for the sports ground. With the lack of funds for sports, Pooja and Manoj also spoke to the minister, who was the MLA for that area, and Manoj had previously attended various events as a guest. The minister agreed to allocate some funds from his MLA fund for sports in Manoj's panchayat. Manoj was filled with gratitude towards Pooja, knowing that expressing this gratitude in front of her wouldn't be well received. With Manoj's support, feelings were rekindling in Pooja, and her emptiness was fading away. She now wanted to meet Manoj daily for some reason, and she was convinced that if what Manoj was doing set off in the right direction, it would lead to extensive social change.

Pooja wanted exactly this—a job that could bring peace to her mind and help people in their reality, guiding them in some way. Manoj's presence had fulfilled this aspect for her again. Every person wants to be connected to something that completes their existence. Both Manoj and Pooja were finding completeness in their incompleteness once again.

While sitting in the car, Pooja told Manoj how life plays games with us. "You might be moving in the right direction, but it creates circumstances that lead you to change your path, and then, years later, you find yourself back on the same road you left because you realize that the path you were on was indeed the right one."

Manoj nodded in agreement.

The next day, Pooja went to see the land designated for the playground. She called Manoj there as well, along with the village head and local representatives. After consulting everyone, she gave final approval for the playground plan so that construction could begin promptly.

After that, Pooja returned to her office, where Manoj was waiting with her. She said to him that if a person truly has talent, they can turn difficult circumstances into their allies. What were once challenges can later become opportunities with courage. "Just look at you; you couldn't join the civil service, but you are now making all these efforts for the youth in your area. I am happy for you."

Manoj quickly replied, "But all the credit goes to you. I had lost hope."

"Pooja, you hadn't lost hope; you just needed support. And as a collector, it's my duty to promote such efforts, so I'm just doing my job," she responded.

Manoj said, "But there could have been another collector in your place who might not take this effort as seriously as you do."

Pooja agreed, "Yes, that's possible; I can't deny that." Then, changing the subject suddenly, Manoj asked, "Pooja, everything is fine, but what have you thought about your family life moving forward?"

As soon as he asked this question, Pooja became irritated. "You have no right to ask this question."

Manoj replied, "I acknowledge that I am responsible for your situation, but I cannot see you alone like this. There should be someone in your life; I see that you are just focused on work and hardly talk to your family. I feel regret seeing you..."

Pooja listened in silence for a moment and then said, "Don't regret; nothing can change now. But I learned something important from my and Ashish's marriage: if you want to exit a marriage, it should not be based on provocation or external reasons. Such separations can lead to regret later. The decision to separate should come with the understanding that our principles and ways of living, our priorities, are oppositional. Priorities can differ, and we can still coexist and love, but we cannot stay together if we are fundamentally opposed to each other. Such a marriage becomes suffocating, and I don't want to be in such relationship. A marriage that takes away your sense of self won't last long. As for family, as you age and find yourself alone, you start to drift away from everyone. Brothers and sisters move on with their lives after marriage. After our parents are gone, who will I look for? After mom and dad, there is hardly anyone who genuinely wants to check in on you every day."

Manoj said, "That's why I say that a progressive society berates marriage, describing it as a rotten relationship system. But is there any other arrangement in society that gives permanence to the relationship between a man and a woman? The day such a stable option emerges, people will stop marrying. But for now, marriage is necessary for a pause, for stability."

Pooja felt a pang at the thought that she could have had a good life with Manoj. The plan for her life included a partner like Manoj, who could provide an opportunity for some social change. Her dreams weren't so grand that she needed to get caught up in the race to earn millions or chase after luxury. Yet, sometimes, one asks for much less from life than their potential, and life doesn't even give that.

Pooja asked Manoj seriously, "If we had married, would everything have been okay?"

Manoj replied, "I can't say. When we were connected, we were in love, and love doesn't carry the burden of responsibilities. That's what makes love exhilarating, but relationships come with the awareness of responsibility, and that can also seem like a burden. That's why I made that decision."

Pooja asked, "But you are managing your marriage; are you doing it out of responsibility or love?"

Manoj fell silent, and at that moment, Pooja's government vehicle driver and guard arrived. They asked if they should drop Manoj home. Pooja looked at Manoj, and he stood up to leave. He walked toward the vehicle, but Pooja still didn't get an answer to the question she wanted to ask him. Just as Manoj was about to get in the car, the guard called out that the madam was also coming, and they would take Manoj along to drop him home.

When Pooja got into the car, Manoj said, "Why are you worrying? I will leave." Pooja replied, "No, I will also go; there's a panchayat meeting, and I will stay there tonight." The collector instructed her stenographers to inform the concerned tehsildar to reach there, stating she would arrive in an hour. Once the madam's order was given, the administrative machinery went into action. Shortly after, Pooja's government vehicle was speeding toward Manoj's village.

The whole way, Pooja was only aware of Manoj's presence; her heart once again longed to be with him. She understood both the price and the possibility of it, but this conflict had taken root in her mind. The conflict was about why she couldn't embrace someone who was once hers if they were not able to be together for some reason.

Being married and being in love can be two different things, and her heart was preparing to give itself another chance based on this reasoning. While caught in this inner conflict, she suddenly found herself at Manoj's doorstep. As he stepped out to go inside, Pooja said, "Think about my question and give me an answer. I will wait."

Hearing Pooja's question, Manoj moved ahead without saying anything, and in the darkness of the night, Pooja's government vehicle pierced the darkness with its headlights.

As Manoj opened his home door, he saw it had been opened from inside. There was Gudiya, with Manoj's daughter laughing in her lap.

Upon seeing them, Manoj was overwhelmed with emotion. After so many days, seeing his daughter, a wave of affection surged within him, and excitedly, he asked Gudiya when she had arrived. "She came this morning. I had the key to the back door, so I came in from there. I knew you must have locked the front door," Gudiya replied. She had prepared food for Manoj, and after a long time, he ate with a happy heart. Manoj thought he would now tell Gudiya everything about the circumstances they had faced and how they had navigated those problems.

Manoj felt a peace in his chest that comes after a terrible storm passes. Gudiya wanted to keep the atmosphere calm and didn't want to stir up any old issues, and Manoj felt the same. After all the chores were done, Gudiya came to the bedside, and by then, the baby was asleep.

As Manoj started speaking, Gudiya suddenly asked, "Who dropped you off?"

Manoj replied, "Pooja came to drop me."

Gudiya became irritated, "While I wasn't here, you were with her, right? You didn't even think of coming home with your wife and child."

Manoj said, "I thought about it many times, but the situation here was so bad that you all would have been troubled."

Gudiya shot back, "Then the situation must still be bad since everything became perfectly fine as soon as we came."

Manoj remained silent, and to change the subject, he turned over to lie down. Gudiya became annoyed. "Do you think I don't understand what's going on? Your friendship with that girl from Delhi is being carried out here. I am not a fool. She is here to break my home after getting her own divorce."

Gudiya said that although the collector sahiba had not given much attention to their marriage in her life but for Gudiya, this relationship was everything, and she would not accept that anyone could come and shake the foundation of this relationship.

Manoj knew that Gudiya felt insecure about Pooja and was fixated on her even after coming back from her parental home. Manoj tried to dispel the misunderstanding that had arisen in Gudiya's mind regarding Pooja.

Manoj: "Pooja has helped us a lot in the meantime; you are unjustly viewing her with suspicion."

Gudiya flared up again and said, "I am not looking at her with suspicion; I am fully convinced that something is going on in her mind. A woman can sense what another woman is thinking."

Manoj: "Gudiya, don't say foolish things; you are not understanding the seriousness of the matter. Never let this slip in front of Pooja, it would hurt her greatly."

Gudiya: "And you don't care about how I feel."

Manoj: "Oh, don't talk nonsense. Instead of standing by me in trouble, you always become a troublemaker. Last time when I was in trouble, you should have been with me, but you made my situation worse and went back to your parental home. Now that you've come back, you've brought this new obsession; you are worlds apart from Pooja. I'm not just playing the flute in front of a buffalo." Saying this, Manoj got up and went to another room. After saying all this in one breath, Manoj realized what he had said, and his words had pierced Gudiya's soul. Manoj had made a grave mistake.

A month had passed, and in the meantime, through marathon-level efforts, a playground had been prepared in Manoj's village, and today the inauguration of that playground was to take place. The minister was the chief guest, and Collector Pooja was also expected to arrive. There was a huge crowd at the playground. All the girls from Manoj's sports academy were present, and Lakhaniya and Baby were overjoyed because their experiences from the state training camp had been consulted in designing the playground, and all arrangements were ensured based on that. Moreover, the security of the playground was ensured in such a way that no objectionable actions could take place there.

In his speech, the minister took all the credit for preparing this playground first for himself because the grant for this playground had been passed from his MLA fund, and he gave the second credit to Collector Pooja and Manoj. Ranveer had also come there that day to flatter the minister, and he was once again reminded that Manoj had surpassed him, but he was helpless to do anything. The event ended with great enthusiasm. As all the guests were leaving, Gudiya approached Pooja. Gudiya had come there with Lakhaniya and Baby. As soon as Pooja saw the child in Gudiya's arms, she took her and asked Gudiya about her well-being. Gudiya softly said, "I want to meet you alone; is that possible?"

For a moment, Pooja was taken aback, but then she quickly composed herself and said, "Yes, tell me where to meet." Gudiya then informed her that Manoj and Chandan would be going to the city in two days to buy kits for the girls, and on that day, Gudiya would come to meet Pooja at her residence.

Pooja replied, "Okay, let me know the time, and I will send a car for you."

Gudiya responded, "No, I will come with Lakhaniya. You have to promise me not to tell Manoj about this." Gudiya was worried that if Pooja refused to meet her or told Manoj about this beforehand, her suspicions would certainly be confirmed. For two days, Pooja was in a dilemma; she understood that Gudiya would come to discuss Manoj.

Two days later, Gudiya arrived at Pooja's place with Lakhaniya. Gudiya made Lakhaniya sit outside and went into Pooja's room alone. Pooja welcomed Gudiya with full respect.

Pooja: "Yes, Gudiya, what did you want to talk about?"

Gudiya began to speak with great courage, "I was very happy when I got married for the first time at the age of 19; I should have been happy to marry such a good man. He was the only son in his family. A woman desires only one thing from her man: that he listens to her carefully, even paying attention to trivial matters. Whether a woman is a high-ranking official or a housewife, they may be in different situations, but their desire from their husbands remains the same: to listen to them.

The man who fulfills this small desire becomes a woman's hero. He was exactly like that for me; he listened to everything I said. Within a few days of our marriage, I felt I had received all the happiness in the world. Then one day he had an accident, and my world collapsed. Just a week into our marriage, and I became an unfortunate widow, a burden on my parental home while people spread rumors that I was inauspicious.

These things carry a lot of weight in villages. Many bizarre people contacted my father during this time, urging him to get me remarried, but due to this unfortunate incident, my father did not want to push me anywhere. After enduring six years of widowhood, Manoj took me in. He married me and gave my life a new direction, dispelling the darkness in my life.

After six years of widowhood, I found a way to live, and now we have a child together. He is our hope. I beg you with folded hands not to let any upheaval come into my settled life; I won't be able to bear it. You hold such a high position; you are such a great personality. I am not even the dust of your feet, perhaps that's why I am so scared, and I plead with you to let Manoj remain only mine." As she spoke, Gudiya sat on the ground and began to wipe her tears with the end of her sari. Pooja had expected this from Gudiya; she had anticipated that Gudiya would say something like this, so she was prepared.

She held Gudiya by the shoulders and lifted her up, looking into her eyes, she said, "Gudiya, once upon a time, Manoj and I studied together; we had a very good friendship. Manoj helped me during my civil service preparation and guided me to reach this level. When you spend a long time with someone, you become sensitive to their joys and sorrows. You start to feel a connection with them as a well-wisher. You will start to feel that way too, but the kind of relationship you are thinking about between me and Manoj is merely a misunderstanding.

Do not view our relationship with suspicion. Manoj studied in Delhi, where co-education is common; boys and girls study together, and it doesn't mean that if a girl talks to a boy, something wrong is happening between them. You can rest assured and don't bring any such foolish thoughts into your mind. You might think that I can say this because I'm living outside my marriage, but please remove that from your mind. I have never liked Manoj. I grew up in cities while he came from a village. Our thoughts, beliefs, society, and culture are all different.

Today, I am a high-ranking government official, while Manoj is still struggling. I belong to a society of officers now, I have a status to maintain. Manoj and I only have an acquaintance, nothing more. Even then, if you keep thinking about this, you will only hurt yourself and ruin your relationship with Manoj.

Manoj is a sensible person and loves you a lot; so, clear your mind of all these thoughts and try to support him in the work he is doing."

Gudiya listened quietly to Pooja.

Pooja: "I am an independent woman, and I have reached this level on my own; no one can become my husband and control me with his commands. That's why my first marriage didn't last; my husband wanted to control me, and nothing could be done against my will. Despite my best efforts, I couldn't save my marriage. When we are in love or a relationship with someone, we expect the same response we want to hear from them, but that doesn't always happen because we are two different individuals, come from different backgrounds, may have different priorities, dreams, and make decisions differently."

"When we begin to understand the acceptance of responses that differ from our expectations in relationships, only then can we truly mature in love. Before that, we are merely companions of convenience. We feel good with our partner only as long as they do what is convenient for us. This was the case with my first husband; he never understood that I only wanted his companionship, but he kept deciding things based on his own convenience. You mustn't make the same mistake of being just a partner of Manoj's convenience. In tough situations, Manoj needs your support even more; in such times, going back to your parental home is not the right decision, Gudiya. A man can feel very lonely.

Gudiya said, "Yes, I did go back, but I did it for my child's future." Pooja replied, "You did the right thing, but there were other ways to explain this to Manoj. I'm saying this as a well-wisher for both of you." Gudiya expressed her viewpoint, "I never made any demands of him or opposed him, but his decision was wrong, which is why I did,what I did.

Pooja-Manoj wanted to become an IAS officer but couldn't; this has created a void within him that repeatedly questions his worth and capability. That's why he now wants to do things where he can prove his worth and achieve results according to his expectations. If you try to stop him, you will endanger your relationship. Sometimes, this inner void makes a person so critical that even if you show him the right path, he will only see reasons for his criticism and for not being loved.

Gudiya said, "So then, we shouldn't offer advice at all, and should remain mute spectators to whatever decisions are made, right or wrong?"

Pooja replied, "No, that's not what I mean. Advice should be given, but timing is crucial. It's important to consider when and where advice is offered. If you keep this in mind, the situation can come under control. Most importantly, you should not let the person feel that their actions will lead to some loss or problems. Instead, if you highlight the benefits of their decision, they become more willing to listen to your opinion. You should also express your doubts and challenges in the middle of those discussions, so they know what difficulties could arise in achieving those results."

Gudiya said, "I will keep your advice in mind, but I want to say one last thing. People want to love someone who gives them freedom, but the very first condition of love is to be bound to someone. How can bondage and freedom coexist? But this is a deep secret; not everyone gets it. Achieving freedom while being bound to someone is a different art, a form of self-control; this self-control is love. If someone is unable to find love out of fear of losing freedom, it means there is a lack of balance in their life. The sooner this understanding comes, the deeper love can grow. Now I must leave; it's getting late." Gudiya concluded her thoughts. Pooja pondered over her words for a moment and then said, "Wait, let me arrange a ride for you."

Gudiya replied, "No, I came with Lakhaniya, and I will leave with him." As Gudiya got up to leave, Pooja said, "Be assured from my side, and stay happy in your family life."

For a few days after this incident, everything remained normal. Manoj and Pooja did not meet each other, and then one day, Manoj decided that he should start taking children to the sports stadium established by the Panchayat for formal training and accelerate the training process. There was a district-level championship at the end of next month, and a national-level championship was to follow in four months. The past seven to eight months had passed only amidst various upheavals. Therefore, Manoj wanted to abandon all other matters and focus on preparing to raise the flag of his sports academy at the district, state, and national levels.

For the level of focus required, it was essential that he completely distance himself from anything that could undermine his inner morale. So, he thought he should meet Pooja once and inform her that he was now completely ready for training with the children. When Manoj arrived at Pooja's office, as usual, she was out in the field somewhere. After waiting for three hours, when Pooja returned, a smile broke out on her face upon seeing Manoj.

Pooja asked, "How are things going?" Manoj then shared all his future plans. In the course of their conversation, Manoj asked Pooja, "I apologize to you." Pooja replied, "For what?" Manoj said, "I found out that Gudiya came to meet you with Lakhaniya; I know what she must have asked you."Pooja responded, "Manoj, when we last met, I asked you a question, and you turned towards home without answering it." Manoj fidgeted because he wanted to avoid answering that question. But Pooja shifted the tone, "You don't need to answer that question now. Love is a process of purification; whenever lust, greed, or cunning tries to dominate, it will be the power of love that purifies this filth. Love transcends the matter of gaining or not gaining a person. Gudiya came to me asking for her husband; I told her that her husband is with her, and I have nothing."

Manoj: Yes, I spoke to her. When I found out why she came to meet you, she told me about your meeting

Pooja: I was yours yesterday, and Gudiya is yours today. I didn't want Gudiya to carry the thought of having any relationship between us into her future life with you. Nothing is more powerful than time; it creates deep wounds and also heals them. I have already healed the wound of parting from you, but I don't want Gudiya to live her life with that wound alongside you. Anyway, there is a difference between love and marriage; love is natural and happens instinctively, and our love happened naturally. But marriage is a social responsibility, a promise. If our love had turned into marriage, perhaps we would both have been bound by responsibility, but that didn't happen. Now Gudiya and your child are that responsibility. Saying this, Pooja fell silent.

After a few moments of silence, Manoj spoke up.

Manoj: How much better it would have been if the lover within us could have turned into husband and wife. Now the lover is separate, and the husband is separate. But every man's life is a game where he cannot remain merely a spectator. He has to play the game forcefully; in life's game, there is no guarantee that playing too defensively will lead to victory, nor is it certain that aggression will make him a winner. Everything depends on circumstances, courage, luck, cooperation, morale, and challenges. This is the lambda value of life. Pintoo used to say this, right?

Pooja: That's true, but life has its own rules, Manoj. When a person climbs up towards success in life, he only sees what he is gaining and does not notice what he is losing. Similarly, when a person falls into despair or sorrow, he only sees what he has not achieved, not what he has already attained. Life does not give you everything; whenever it gives something, it already decides what it will take in return. I had to get this position, this prestige, and in return, you were left behind, happiness was left behind, and family was left behind. This was the plan of life.

# Chapter 29

With Pooja's help, Manoj had started preparing Lakhaniya and Baby for the upcoming event, and the academy had also resumed practice for other children. When practice began, Pooja came there to encourage all the players. Everyone was very happy, and a new enthusiasm blossomed within everyone. Small successes are important because they pave the way for a bigger victory and keep morale high. At that time, Manoj expressed his gratitude to Pooja in front of everyone.

Manoj: If you hadn't been here Pooja, this would not have been manageable.

Pooja: I didn't do anything; this is all your vision, your effort. I get a salary for this work from the government. I am a public servant, and solving people's problems is my duty and my inspiration.

Manoj: Then why can't everyone become such public servants, Pooja? I asked you this before, but you didn't give a precise reason. The matter was deferred. You have a habit of not accepting your good qualities in front of everyone; perhaps you fear that those good habits may slip away. If you share some of these with these children, maybe it will help many of them in their lives.

Upon hearing this, everyone present smiled; Pooja felt shy but then responded to Manoj's words with a slight smile.

Pooja: It's not that I don't acknowledge my good qualities. Yes, I do make sure that I don't become overconfident out of admiration for them. Overconfidence is very dangerous and can cause severe harm. Anyway, I will now answer the crucial question about being a public servant. I might be wrong, but I feel that the rigorous preparation for Preparation for civil services makes the candidate less friendly with society, family and friends. The pressure to succeed in the examination is so great that the student remains focused solely on it and desires selection under any circumstances. They even distance themselves from essential family activities, limited social interactions. Initially, this behavior is confined to their exams and studies for achieving their goal, but even after selection, this process continues in the student's personality. Preparing for civil services mostly makes a candidate goal-oriented. To achieve this, the candidate needs to mold their personality into being highly controlled and limiting their interactions. Even a civil servant interacts primarily to accomplish a specific predefined goal, as their role demands it. If you remain overly interactive, you may find yourself surrounded by unnecessary troubles and people's problems, which can hinder you from achieving your objectives.That's why a student who has become a selected officer places more emphasis on the comforts, prestige, and security of their job rather than being sensitive to public concerns and interactions and only does what is necessary to keep the government records and work clean.

In such a situation, it becomes extremely contradictory after selection for government service that we expect that government officer to be highly social when he has become accustomed to a-social life as a student. It is equally worth noting that a unidimensional and single-minded student rarely succeeds in this examination. Therefore, the option of avoiding this kind of life during civil service preparation is very limited for serious students, and they must become accustomed to a tendency where they confine themselves only to studies. There may be exceptions of those who joked their way to selection.

Manoj: Your argument is generally valid, but there are certainly exceptions like you. You were very social during your preparation, remained very social after selection, and are still working with complete dedication towards public concerns. There are such officers, but it is not typical behavior; it is due to the high morale and personal values of those officers.

The conversation continued for quite a while until Pooja left. Manoj knew in his heart that this was perhaps his last meeting with Pooja and that it was also not appropriate for either of them to meet continuously in the future. However, they both wanted to keep this meeting as a good memory so that if they ever met again, it would bring them joy rather than any kind of resentment. Sometimes, relationships have a healthy lifespan, and they should reach a conclusion within a limit; otherwise, they can become distorted. Respecting the relationship is very important.

Anyway, Manoj now had a different challenge ahead. He was preparing Lakhaniya and Baby with all his strength for the upcoming qualifying round of the National Games. Lakhaniya and Baby were not allowing any entanglement in their minds this time and were preparing with full vigor. Other children from Manoj's academy had also started to raise the flag in district, inter-district, and regional level competitions again.

One night, Manoj invited Lakhaniya, Baby, and Chandan to his home for dinner. By inviting them for dinner, he wanted to quell that inner fear that might be hiding somewhere in Lakhaniya or Baby. He also wanted to express himself in front of Gudiya. Therefore, there could be no better way than this.

During dinner, Manoj said: The past few times have been very difficult for all of us; many misunderstandings arose, many wrong decisions were made, and many unwanted problems came our way, leading to poor decisions. But despite all these problems, we are still together, and therein lies our strength. We have all hurt each other in one way or another, made many mistakes, and made compromises in dire situations that shook our self-respect. But it is not true that compromises are always bad; sometimes, they are very helpful for improving situations and going through bad phases of life.

However, one should always keep in mind that compromises should be made, and they should only happen due to circumstances. Compromises should never stem from willpower. Compromises should never be made to halt progress. They should be made to wait for favorable times, to take a leap backward to take a leap forward again, and to help oneself after falling. Shri Krishna decided to go to Dwarka to save the lives and properties of the citizens of Mathura from Jarasandha's attacks. Neither Krishna would remain in Mathura nor Jarasandha would attack there. Then, when the time was right, Krishna, with the help of Pandav son Bhima, succeeded in ending Jarasandha's life.

A few days later, Manoj left for Lucknow with the girls for the state-level competition. In this race, Lakhaniya and Baby were once again meeting the same faces that they had seen the last time when they returned from the hostel after facing a crushing defeat. It is undoubtedly an uncomfortable situation to face those who have witnessed your decline, but for those who are determined to fight back, they must eventually confront those who were there during their tough times. This is essential because these people become witnesses to future victories and advocates of struggle. When critics have lost all hope in you due to your previous poor performance, a true athlete carves out a place for themselves with courage and determination.

As always, Lakhaniya and Baby were running in their respective segments. So they were confident this time and as a result of this, both of them ran with such intensity that they set national records in their segments and qualified for the national games happening in two months. The critics were silenced, and they were forced to rethink what it was about these two girls that was turning them into dark horses once again. The next day, the newspapers were filled once again with stories of Lakhaniya, Baby, and Manoj. Manoj and his team wanted to give their best performance once again.

Through experience, Manoj had understood that if someone chooses a field that aligns with their natural abilities, they cannot be stopped from excelling. Lakhaniya and Baby had innate talent, which Manoj had honed.

After qualifying for the state, Lakhaniya and Baby went back to the state hostel for training camp, but this time, Manoj maintained contact with both girls and continuously checked on their preparations. The girls were also fully focused on their practice during the camp. Manoj explained to them that victory in sports comes not only from physical efficiency but also from mental strength. Therefore, no matter what happens, they should not allow themselves to break under any circumstances.

However, things are not always that easy. As one moves towards their goal, obstacles also increase rapidly. In the sports hostel, Lakhaniya's old boyfriend, Rakesh, was looking for an opportunity to take revenge. He wanted to ruin Lakhaniya because Manoj and Lakhaniya had humiliated him at a restaurant, leading to the collapse of his marriage.

During his stay at the hostel, Rakesh made many attempts to harass Lakhaniya. He tried to damage her reputation by filing false complaints with the management, but this time the situation was entirely different. Lakhaniya and Baby were record-holding athletes in the state-level games, so the management saw them as winners. Both girls were highly focused on their goals and were distancing themselves from any controversies.

With victories in the national games, they were set to qualify for the upcoming Commonwealth Games. This was a significant opportunity for both to participate in international competitions, akin to a grand dream.

Manoj had explained to both girls that sometimes it's better to walk away from a dispute rather than fight. Life can be easier when you listen to your inner voice rather than external noise. Sticking to this principle, the day of the national games arrived for both girls. A few days before the nationals, Manoj also reached the hostel and was in regular contact with the girls.

On the day of the nationals, both girls were ready and arrived at the ground to meet Manoj. After discussing all the preparations, they went to their room to grab their sports bags. They were going to the track with these bags. Meanwhile, Rakesh quietly sat at the edge of the spectator area. Two boys sitting in front of him appeared to be staff from the hostel, and their conversation revealed that they had poisoned someone's energy drink at someone's suggestion in exchange for five thousand rupees, and they were arguing about how to split that money.

Hearing their conversation, Manoj thought of Lakhaniya and rushed back to the hostel. He found Baby just below the hostel.

Manoj: "Did you drink anything, Baby?"

Baby: "No, brother, but what happened?"

Manoj: "Where is Lakhaniya?"

Baby: "Lakhaniya went to the bathroom; she should be back soon." Just as Manoj was about to explain everything to Baby, a girl came running and informed them that Lakhaniya was vomiting in her room. Manoj and Baby rushed to the hostel room, and Lakhaniya was vomiting repeatedly. Manoj understood the situation immediately. He decided to take Lakhaniya to the doctor right away and told Baby to go to the track and complete her race since her race was first.

Lakhaniya's race was scheduled for two hours later, so he left with her to see the doctor. Hearing Manoj, Baby made her way to the ground, but her mind was filled with concern for Lakhaniya. She felt restless on the track, but the announcement for the race preparation had been made. Meanwhile, Manoj arrived at the hospital with Lakhaniya. He had also called Pooja to inform her and request help; In turn, she called the hospital administration to ensure Lakhaniya's treatment. With Pooja's authoritative call, a doctor and his team immediately began treating Lakhaniya. The doctor was treating her and repeatedly inducing vomiting.

On the other hand, the race for the national games had begun, and Baby was running with all her might. This time, she was competing against the best players from across the country. She felt weak in the final moments, but then she remembered Manoj's words: no matter what happens, she should not lose hope until the very end and seize every opportunity to bring victory to herself. Life often prepares you for the most critical moments. This is the ultimate test of life.

As the race started with the sound of the gun, Baby pushed her legs with all her strength. She ran like lightning, not looking at anyone but focusing solely on the finish line. However, the competition was very tough today. Other top players were also running alongside, and they all had strong morale. As the final round of the race was about to end, Baby was still behind many players despite giving her all.

For the last round, she gathered every ounce of strength she had left and began to run like a rocket. The tension in her thighs showed how fiercely she was striving for the final round. Yet, despite all her efforts, another player was still ahead of Baby in the final moments. But just then, history was made; with a microsecond's difference, Baby crossed the finish line first, winning the race and qualifying for the upcoming Commonwealth Games.

In the hospital, Lakhaniya was unconscious. The doctor stated that due to the effects of poison, the lower part of Lakhaniya's body had stopped functioning. Several hours had passed, and Manoj was still at the hospital. Chandan, Gudiya, Baby, and Pooja had all arrived as well. Lakhaniya's family members were also present. Lakhaniya's dream of participating in the National Games had remained unfulfilled. Based on Manoj's complaint, Rakesh and the two hostel staff members were arrested for administering poison.

The next day brought a new sunrise, and its meaning was different for Baby and Lakhaniya. While newspapers presented Baby as a heroine, Lakhaniya was portrayed as a victim of a crime. Baby's victory caught the attention of prominent national sports journalists. She became the topic of discussion about how a girl who once sold vegetables and did labor work in her village had emerged as a national champion.

Lakhaniya's story also made headlines, highlighting how an athlete's career was deliberately sabotaged out of revenge. Several feature articles about Baby, Lakhaniya, and Manoj's journey were published in renowned newspapers across the country. These media reports reached policymakers, emphasizing how a coach had prepared athletes at the village panchayat level and brought transformative changes to sports development in the area.

The people of the area began to see sports as a measure of success. Victories lend legitimacy to any struggle, and the triumph of Manoj and his athletes validated their efforts. While the incident with Lakhaniya was unfortunate, there was no way to undo it. Lakhaniya survived, but her dream was shattered.

A few days later, the Union Ministry of Sports issued a statement announcing the launch of the Panchayat Sports Development Scheme to promote sports at the grassroots level. Under this initiative, funds would be allocated annually for the development of sports, providing young people with opportunities to participate and access basic training infrastructure at the panchayat level. The scheme aimed to identify talented youth across the country who could represent India in national and international sports competitions. To ensure effective implementation of the scheme, the ministry appointed the dynamic and honest officer Pooja Shriprakash as its director and Manoj as an advisor.

# Chapter 30

Three years later, the Asian Games were being held, and all eyes were on the Indian athlete representing the country. With the sound of the starting gun, the Indian athlete sprinted for the 200-meter race, and before anyone could fully grasp what was happening, history had already been made. In just a few moments, the gold medal for the 200-meter race at the Asian Games was in India's hands.

At that very moment, an Indian TV journalist covering sports began speaking on camera:

"Lakhaniya Kumari has created a new history today by winning the gold medal in the 200-meter event at the Asian Games. Just two years ago, during the national games, a fellow athlete, out of revenge, had poisoned her. The poison had caused her legs to stop functioning, and she was bedridden for several months. But today, the way Lakhaniya Kumari has claimed victory at the Asian Games once again proves that with determination and mental strength, any dream can be achieved. Circumstances can be turned in one's favour."

www.ingramcontent.com/pod-product-compliance
Lightning Source LLC
Chambersburg PA
CBHW021523150726
47990CB00006B/2069